THIS DIARY BELONGS TO:

Nikki J. Maxwell

PRIVATE & CONFIDENTIAL

If found, please return to ME for REWARD!

(NO SNOOPING ALLOWED!! ☹)

Rachel Renée Russell

DORK diaries

Tales from a
NOT-SO-
Fabulous Life

Aladdin

New York London Toronto Sydney

To my daughter, Nikki,
who tried her hardest to be the best
little ant in the ant colony, when all along
she was a beautiful butterfly.

☞ ALADDIN * An imprint of Simon & Schuster Children's Publishing Division 1230 Avenue of the Americas, New York, NY 10020 * Copyright © 2009 by Rachel Renée Russell * All rights reserved, including the right of reproduction in whole or in part in any form. ALADDIN and related logo are registered trademarks of Simon & Schuster, Inc. * Designed by Lisa Vega * The text of this book was set in Skippy Sharp. * Manufactured in the United States of America * 1110 MTN
Library of Congress Control Number 2008048567
ISBN 978-1-4169-8006-3 (POB)
ISBN 978-1-4169-8655-3 (eBook)
ISBN 978-1-4424-2678-8 (Scholastic paperback)

ACKNOWLEDGMENTS

I would like to thank everyone who helped to make my dream become a reality:

Liesa Abrams, my fantastic editor, for bringing great passion to this project and loving it as much as I did.

Lisa Vega, my super art director, for her keen eye and never-ending patience.

Daniel Lazar at Writers House, my wonderful agent who NEVER sleeps. Thank you for your genius in realizing the potential of this book when it was merely fifty rambling pages about a quirky girl and her fairy godmother. Also, my agents Maja Nikolic, Cecilia de la Campa, and Angharad Kowal at Writers House who are handling foreign rights.

Nikki Russell and Leisl Adams, my very talented assistant artists, whose hard work helped to bring this in under deadline.

Doris Edwards, my mom, for being there through thick and thin and always reassuring me that my writing was funny, even when it probably wasn't.

My daughters, Erin and Nikki Russell, for their love and encouragement.

Arianna Robinson, Mikayla Robinson, and Sydney James, my tween-age nieces, for being the sweetest, most fab, and totally brutal critique partners an author could wish for.

Sometimes I wonder if my mom is BRAIN DEAD. Then there are days when I know she is.

Like today.

The drama started this morning when I casually asked if she would buy me one of those cool new iPhones that do almost everything. I considered it a necessity of life, second only to maybe oxygen.

What better way to clinch a spot in the CCP (Cute, Cool & Popular) group at my new private school, Westchester Country Day, than by dazzling them with a wicked new cell.

Last year, it seemed like I was the ONLY student in my ENTIRE middle school who didn't have one ☹. So I bought an older, used phone supercheap on eBay.

It was bigger than what I wanted, but I figured I couldn't go wrong for the clearance price of only $12.99.

I put my telephone in my locker and spread the word that everyone could now call me with all the JUICY gossip on my NEW telephone! Then I counted down the minutes before my social life started heating up.

I got really nervous when two of the CCP girls came walking down the hall in my direction chatting on their cell phones.

←ME

They came right over to my locker and started acting superfriendly. Then they invited me to sit with them at lunch and I was like, "Umm . . . okay." But deep down inside I was jumping up and down and doing my Snoopy "happy dance."

Then things got really strange. They said they had heard about my new $600 Juicy Couture designer cell phone and that everyone (meaning the rest of the CCP crew) couldn't wait to see it.

I was about to explain that I had said "juicy gossip on my *new* phone" NOT "new gossip on my *Juicy* phone," but I never got a chance because, unfortunately, my telephone starting ringing. Very abnormally loudly. I was trying my best to ignore it,

but both of the CCP girls were staring at me like, "Well, aren't you going to answer it?!"

Obviously, I didn't want to answer it because I had a really bad feeling they were going to be a little disappointed when they actually saw my phone.

So I just stood there praying that it would stop ringing, but it didn't. And pretty soon, everyone in the hallway was staring at me too.

Finally, I gave in, snatched open my locker, and answered the phone. Mainly to stop that AWFUL ringing.

I was like, "Hello? Umm . . . sorry. Wrong number."

And when I turned around, both of the CCP girls were running down the hall screaming, "Make it go away! Make it go away!" I guessed it probably meant they DIDN'T want me to sit with them at lunch anymore, which was a very disappointing thing.

The most important lesson I learned last year was that having a CRUDDY phone—or NONE at all— can totally RUIN your social life. While the CCP girls regularly FORGET to do their homework, not a single one would be caught dead without her cell phone. Which was why I was nagging my mom about buying me an iPhone.

I've tried saving up my own money to buy one, but it was impossible to do. Mainly because I'm an artist and TOTALLY ADDICTED to drawing!

4

Like, if I don't do it every day, I'll go NUTZ!

I spend ALL of my cash on sketchbooks, pencils, pens, art camp, and other stuff. Hey, I'm so BROKE, I have a milkshake on layaway at McDonald's!

Anyway, when mom came home from the mall with a special back-to-school present for me, I was pretty sure I knew what it was.

She rambled on and on about how my attending a new private school was going to be a "stressful time of tremendous personal growth" and how my best "coping mechanism" would be to "communicate" my "thoughts and feelings."

I was absolutely ECSTATIC

because you can communicate with a

NEW CELL PHONE!

Right?! ☺

I kind of zoned out on most of what my mom was

5

saying because I was DAYDREAMING about all of
the cool ring tones,
music, and movies
I was going to
download. It was
going to be LOVE
AT FIRST SIGHT!

But after my mom *finally* finished her little speech,
she smiled really big, hugged me,
and handed me a BOOK.

I opened it and FRANTICALLY
flipped through the pages,
figuring that maybe she had
hidden my new cell phone inside.

It made perfect sense at the time because all the
advertisements said it was *the* thinnest model on
the market.

But slowly it dawned on me that my mom had NOT gotten me a cell phone, and my so-called present was just a stupid little book! ☹

Talk about major HEARTBREAK!

Then I noticed that ALL the pages of the book were BLANK.

I was like, OH. NO. SHE. DIDN'T!

My mom had given me two things: a DIARY and irrefutable evidence she IS, in fact,

CLINICALLY BRAIN DEAD!!

Absolutely no one writes their most intimate feelings and deep, dark secrets in a diary anymore! WHY?!

Because just one or two people knowing all your BIZ could completely ruin your reputation.

You're supposed to post this kind of juicy stuff online in your BLOG so MILLIONS can read it!!!

Only a TOTAL DORK would be caught WRITING in a DIARY!!

This is THE worst present I have ever received in my entire life! I wanted to yell at the top of my lungs:

"Mom, I don't need a STUPID book with 288 BLANK pages!!"

What I NEED is to be able to "communicate" my "thoughts and feelings" to my friends using my very own cell phone.

Wait! Silly me. I keep forgetting. I don't have any friends. YET. But that could change overnight, and I need to be prepared. With a shiny, new cell!

In the meantime, I will NOT write in this diary again.

NEVER! EVER!!

Okay. I know I said I'd never write in this diary again. I meant it at the time. I'm definitely not the kind of girl who curls up with a diary and a box of Godiva chocolates to write a bunch of really sappy stuff about my dreamy boyfriend, my first kiss, or my overwhelming ANGST about the HORRIFIC discovery that I'm a PRINCESS of a small French-speaking principality and now worth MILLIONS.

THIS IS SO <u>NOT</u> ME!

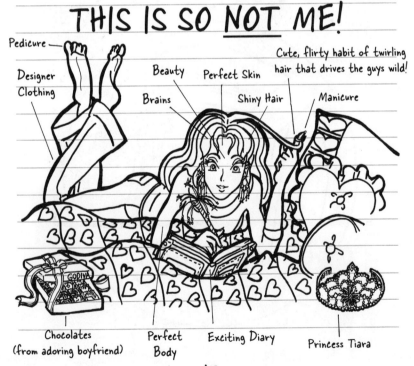

Pedicure

Designer Clothing

Beauty

Perfect Skin

Brains

Shiny Hair

Cute, flirty habit of twirling hair that drives the guys wild!

Manicure

Chocolates (from adoring boyfriend)

Perfect Body

Exciting Diary

Princess Tiara

MY LIFE TOTALLY SUCKS!!

All day I wandered around my new school like a zombie in lip gloss. Not a single person bothered to say hi.

THIS IS ME!

MOST OF THE TIME I FEEL INVISIBLE!

How am I supposed to fit in at a snobby prep school like Westchester Country Day?! This place has a Starbucks in the cafeteria!

I wish my dad had NEVER been awarded a bug extermination contract from this school.

They can take their little pity scholarship and give it to someone who wants and needs it, because I sure DON'T!

It's way past midnight, and I'm about to freak out because I still don't have my homework done. The assignment is for Honors English Lit and we're reading *A Midsummer Night's Dream* by Shakespeare. I was kind of surprised, because I didn't know he wrote teen chick lit.

It's about a mischievous fairy named Puck, who tries to break up a really cute couple lost in an enchanted forest.

Then, this guy with a donkey head crashes a big fairy party and hooks up with their queen. Pretty weird stuff!

PAR-TAY!!

Our homework assignment is to complete three essay questions about PUCK:

1. Would you consider Puck the protagonist of the play? Why or why not?

2. How do Puck's personality and actions set the mood of the play?

3. Use your imagination and provide either a detailed physical description or a drawing of Puck.

The first two questions weren't that hard, and I finished them in no time at all. However, the third question threw me for a loop.

I didn't have the slightest idea what Puck looked like.

But I tried to imagine him with cute little pointy ears and AS HOT AS :

NICK JONAS ➚

14

CORBIN BLEU   JUSTIN TIMBERLAKE

I was also dying to know if having a messed-up name like Puck had completely RUINED his life.

I bet the popular kids at his school called him "Puke," "Schmuck," "Yuck," or something worse.

POOR PUCK ☹!!

I tried to go to that educational website "Wiki-something-or-other" that everyone plagiarizes to find a picture of Puck.

But I couldn't remember the name of it and was too lazy to Google it.

I was really surprised to hear a knock on my bedroom door this late at night, and I assumed it was my six-year-old sister, Brianna.

About a week ago, she lost one of her front teeth and buried it in the backyard to see if it would grow. She is FOREVER doing crazy-weird stuff like that.

My mom says it's because she's still a little kid. But I personally think it's because she has the IQ of a box of crayons.

As a little joke, I told Brianna the tooth fairy collected teeth from children all over the world and then Super Glued them together to make dentures for old people.

I explained that she was in BIG TROUBLE with the tooth fairy, seeing as she had dug a hole and buried her tooth somewhere out in the backyard.

The funniest part was that Brianna TOTALLY believed me. She actually dug up half of Mom's flower garden trying to find her tooth.

Since then Brianna has been paranoid that the tooth fairy is going to sneak into her room in the middle of the night and pull out ALL her teeth to make dentures.

But my prank kind of backfired, because now she absolutely REFUSES to use the bathroom at night unless I first check to make sure the tooth fairy is not hiding behind the shower curtain or under the bath towels.

And if I'm not quick enough, Brianna will have a little "accident" right on my bedroom carpet.

B-BUT, WHAT IF THE **TOOTH FAIRY** IS HIDING IN THERE?! **OOPS...!!**

MY LITTLE SISTER, BRIANNA

ACCIDENT! ☹

Unfortunately, I had to learn the hard way that (contrary to the TV commercial) Carpet Fresh DOES NOT remove all odors.

Lucky for me, it wasn't Brianna at my door, but my parents.

MOM

DAD

Before I could say, "Come in," they just kind of barged in like they always do, which really irritated me, because this is supposed to be MY room! And as an American citizen, I have a constitutional right to PRIVACY, which they keep invading.

The next time my parents and Brianna come rollin' up in here, I'm gonna scream,

"Hey! Why don't y'all just MOVE IN?!"

Anyway, my parents said they were surprised to see that I was still up doing homework, and they wanted to know how things were going at school.

It was really strange, because just as I was about to answer, I had a total meltdown right on the spot and burst into tears.

My parents were shocked and stared at me and then at each other. Finally, Mom hugged me and said, "My poor little Boo-Boo!" which only made me feel WORSE.

Not fitting in at school was bad enough. But now I had to suffer the additional humiliation of being the only fourteen-year-old *still* being called "little Boo-Boo"! Suddenly my dad's face lit up.

"Hey, I've got a great idea! We know you've been under a lot of stress lately with our move and your new school. I bet if we posted some positive affirmations all around the house, it would help you adjust. You think?"

I was like, "Okay, Dad, THIS is what I think: It's a STUPID idea! Like sticky notes with corny sayings on them will solve my problem of being a TOTAL

LOSER at school. You wanna know what else I think? The article I read about bug extermination chemicals killing off brain cells is probably true!"

But I just said it inside my head, so no one else heard it but me.

My parents kept staring at me, and it was starting to creep me out. Finally, after what seemed like forever, my mom smiled and said, "Honey, just remember, we love you! And if you need us, we're right down the hall."

They walked back to their bedroom, and for several minutes, I could hear their muffled voices. I guessed that they were probably discussing whether or not I should be committed to a mental hospital right then or first thing in the morning.

Since it was so late, I decided to finish my Puck assignment during study hall.

I wonder if you still have to hand in homework when you're locked up in a PSYCHO WARD?

WEDNESDAY, SEPTEMBER 4

My new issue of *That's So Hot!* magazine says the secret to happiness is the four Fs:

Friends, Fun, Fashion & Flirting

But, unfortunately, the closest I've ever gotten to "friends, fun, fashion, and flirting" is having a locker right next to MacKenzie Hollister.

She's THE most popular girl in the eighth grade.

Lucky me! ☹

I had just finished fighting my way through the crowded hallways to get to my locker and had almost been trampled alive.

Then, suddenly, as if by magic, the huge mob of students parted right down the center, just like the Red Sea.

That's when I first saw MacKenzie strutting down

the hallway like it was the runway of a Paris fashion show or something.

She had blonde hair and blue eyes and was dressed like she had just left a photo shoot for the cover of *Teen Vogue.*

And everyone (except me) immediately fell under her powerful hypnotic spell and totally lost their minds.

"What's up, MacKenzie!"

"You look hot, MacKenzie!"

"Are you coming to my party this weekend, MacKenzie?"

"Love your shoes, MacKenzie!"

"Will you marry me, MacKenzie?"

"You'll NEVER guess who has a crush on you, MacKenzie!"

"Is that *another* designer purse, MacKenzie?"

"Fabulous hair today, MacKenzie!"

"I'll pluck out my eye with a pencil and eat it with a Spam and mustard sandwich IF ONLY you'll sit with me at lunch today, MacKenzie!"

Which also proves my theory that there's ALWAYS at least ONE seriously mentally ill WEIRDO in EVERY middle school across America!

It was "MacKenzie! MacKenzie! MacKenzie!" When she walked up to the locker right next to mine, I knew then and there I was going to have a VERY bad school year.

Being so close to the radiance of her awesome yet sickening perfection just made me feel like a humongous LOSER. And it didn't help that she was HOGGING most of my personal space ☹!!

Hey, it wasn't like I was jealous of her or anything. I mean, how totally juvenile would THAT be?!

Between classes, MacKenzie and her friends are

forever standing right in front of MY locker, "GGG-ing."

That means:

GIGGLING, GOSSIPING, AND GLOSSING

And whenever I get up the nerve to say, "Excuse me, but I really need to get into my locker," she just ignores me or rolls her eyes and says stuff like, "Annoying much?" or "What's HER problem?"

And I'm like, "Hey, girlfriend! I don't have no STINKIN' problem!"

But I just say it inside my head, so no one really hears it except me.

However, deep down I'm troubled and ashamed that a tiny part of me—a very dark and primitive side—would totally LOVE to be best friends with MacKenzie!

And I find that part of myself SO disgusting . . . I could . . . VOMIT!

But on a much happier note, I'm really into lip gloss too.

My favorite one right now is Krazy Kissalicious Strawberry Crush Glitterati.

It's yummy and tastes just like strawberry cheesecake.

Unfortunately, no supercute hunk (like Brandon Roberts, the guy who sits in front of me in my biology class) has developed a huge crush on me and fallen in love with my fabulous glossy lips, like in all of those KRAZY KISSALICIOUS television commercials.

But, hey! It could happen!

In the meantime, I've decided to try and enjoy my single status.

Oh, I almost forgot! Dad is supposed to pick me up after school today to take me to my dentist appointment.

PLEASE, PLEASE, PLEASE don't let him pick me up in his work van with the five-foot-long plastic roach on top.

I would absolutely DIE if anyone found out I only attend this school due to his bug extermination contract!

☹!!

MacKenzie and her snobby friends are about to get on my last nerve! They're always making NASTY comments about any girl who wanders within six feet of them. I mean, who do they think they are?

THE FASHION POLICE?!

"HI, SWEETIE! YOU'RE UNDER ARREST FOR A FELONY FASHION VIOLATION!"

Today, in under one minute, MacKenzie gave out the following scathing fashion commentary while applying her lip gloss:

"Don't you need a LICENSE to be that UGLY?"

"That outfit would be perfect for Goodwill. If she knows what's GOOD for her, she WILL burn it."

"OMG! I bought that exact same sweater she's wearing! For my dog, from PetSmart."

"What's that awful STANK?! She's supposed to spray on the perfume, not marinate in it."

"She has SO much acne, she uses a special makeup brand. It's called Why Bother."

"What's up with her new hairstyle? It looks like a small mammal made a nest in her hair, had babies, and died!"

"She thinks she's SO cute. She's just living proof that manure can actually grow legs and walk."

To call MacKenzie a "mean girl" would be an understatement. She's VICIOUS! She's a PIT BULL in glittery eye shadow and Jimmy Choo flip-flops!

I think I've finally figured out why I don't fit in at this school. I need a new designer wardrobe from one of those really expensive teen shops at the mall.

You know, the ones where the salesgirls dress like Hannah Montana and have pierced belly buttons, blond highlights, and phony smiles.

But what drives me INSANE is their nasty habit of unexpectedly snatching open the curtain of your dressing room and popping their head inside when you're like HALF NAKED. It's enough to make you want to slap those blond highlights right out of their hair.

And when you look in the mirror, you can obviously see that the outfit looks HORRIBLE on you. But those salesgirls just smile really big and act cute and perky and LIE TO YOUR FACE by saying the outfit (1) looks totally fabulous, (2) brings out your natural skin tones, and (3) complements your eye color.

They'll tell you this EVEN if you're trying on one of those huge green lawn-size HEFTY TRASH BAGS!

"HON! THAT LOOKS SO-O-O-O-O CUTE ON YOU!"

ME (WEARING A TRASH BAG)

I also HATE clothes that are "SNOBBY CHIC."

It's when the exact same outfit looks TOTALLY different on two very similar girls. The more popular you are at school, the BETTER it looks on you, and the more unpopular you are, the WORSE it looks on you. I can't tell you HOW a snobby chic outfit mysteriously knows all of this personal stuff about you, but it obviously DOES!

WHY I HATE SNOBBY CHIC FASHIONS!

COOL SNOBBY CHIC OUTFIT AT THE MALL!

POPULAR GIRL

UNPOPULAR GIRL

The SNOBBY CHIC phenomenon is quite a mind-boggling thing. Hopefully, Congress will allocate funding for scientists to study it, along with how socks mysteriously disappear from the dryer. But, until then, BUYER BEWARE 🙁!

Anyway, after my mom buys me a designer wardrobe, I'm going to walk right up to MacKenzie and her little entourage and tell them off really good.

But before I say anything, I'm going to put my hands on my hips and do that neck-roll thing like Tyra Banks, just to show them how much attitude I really have.

Tyra says every girl must find her own inner beauty deep down inside and ignore all the HATERS. She's SO sweet and a wonderful role model!

Although, I have to admit, she's kind of SCARY on *America's Next Top Model*.

Especially when she's screaming stuff at those poor contestants like, "You FAT, worthless WANNA-BES! You will NEVER, EVER make it in the modeling industry like I did! You have NO idea how much I've BLED and SUFFERED! And wipe that SMIRK off yo' face before I SLAP it off!"

Then she starts crying hysterically and popping Tic Tac breath mints.

I just LOVE that girl!

I've decided that I'm going to tell MacKenzie right to her face (on like maybe the last day of school) that just because she and her clones dress like

FASHIONISTAS,

they do NOT have the right to say really mean things about other people.

"People" being the girls whose moms make them shop at JCPenney, Sears, Target, and Wal-Mart.

Girls like . . . well, ME!

Okay. It's NOT a big secret that the clothes from those stores AREN'T as hot as the clothes from the mall.

And yes, it's a huge inconvenience (and a definite

turnoff) to have to walk through the "OLD
Ladies," "FAT Ladies" and "PREGNANT Ladies"
departments to get to the one for "TEENS" . . .

No wonder most girls prefer those fancy teen shops
in the mall!

FINDING THE TEEN DEPARTMENT

My mom says it really doesn't matter where your clothes come from as long as they're clean. Right?

WRONG!!

I wish I had a dollar for every time I've heard MacKenzie shriek, "OMG! WHERE are these PATHETIC girls buying such HIDEOUS clothes?! I'd come to school butt naked before I would EVER buy my fashions from a store that sells LAWN MOWERS!"

To be honest, I didn't know the stores I shopped at sold lawn mowers. And even if they do, big fat hairy deal.

It's not like the clothes smell like a lawn mower or something. At least, I hadn't noticed it.

The next time I go shopping, I'm going to sniff the clothing before I buy anything, just to make sure.

I'm also going to wear a hat, wig, sunglasses, and phony mustache so no one will recognize me.

WHATEVER!!

My mom and dad are driving me NUTS! In the past 72 hours, they have posted all over the house 139 positive affirmations on rainbow-colored sticky notes that say really stupid things like:

> "Be your OWN best friend. Invite YOURSELF over for a sleepover!"

Unfortunately, I never got a chance to read the one they stuck in the toaster slot thingy because it caught on fire when I tried to make a strawberry Pop-Tart for breakfast.

I had to dump my glass of orange juice on the sticky note to put it out.

And after that, the toaster started melting, shooting blue electrical sparks, and making a loud, angry noise like:

GRRRRRRAAAAAAAGGGG!!

I'm thinking we're probably going to need a new one.

But what was really SCARY was that our house could have actually burnt to the ground. All because my parents stuck a sticky note in the toaster slot thingy.

I know my mom and dad mean well, but sometimes they're an

EMBARRASSMENT!

I'm already dreading that the weekend is almost over and I have to go back to school tomorrow. It's been one whole week and I still haven't made a single friend. I've got this . . . OVERWHELMING . . . sense of loneliness sitting in the pit of my stomach like a . . . big, fat, poisonous . . . TOAD!

ME BEING OVERWHELMED BY THE BIG, FAT, POISONOUS TOAD OF LONELINESS

I'm seriously thinking about asking my parents to let me move back to the city and live with my grandma so I can attend my old school.

I'll admit the school wasn't perfect. But I'd give

anything to hang out with my friends from art class again. I really, really miss them ☹!

Anyway, my grandma lives in one of those apartment buildings for elderly people "who are young at heart and committed to leading a full and active life." So she's up on ALL the latest fads and stuff.

She's also a little wacky (okay, A LOT WACKY) and totally addicted to the game show *The Price Is Right*.

Last year Grandma bought a computer from the Home Shopping Network to help her train to be a contestant on *The Price Is Right*.

Now she spends most of her spare time on her computer, memorizing the suggested retail prices of all the major grocery store brands.

She plans to use all her research and game strategies to write a how-to manual called *The Price Is Right for Morons*.

Grandma says her book could be bigger than *Harry Potter.*

MY GRANDMA

I didn't think being on a game show took any special skills, but she told me you had to train like you would for the Super Bowl.

She took a few sips of her energy drink, stared at me real seriouslike, and whispered, "Sweetie, when life presents challenges, you can be either a CHICKEN or a CHAMPION. The choice is YOURS!"

Then she started humming "Girls Just Want to Have Fun" really loud.

I was like, JUST GREAT! Grandma is finally going SENILE! Doesn't she understand that some things in life you're STUCK with and powerless to change?! Jeez!

But I have to admit she has gotten pretty good at *The Price Is Right*. The last few times I saw her play along with the game show, she got every single price correct! It was amazing because she would have won like $549,321 in cash and prizes, including three cars, a boat, a trip for two to Niagara Falls, and a lifetime supply of Depends adult diapers.

I gave her a big hug and said, "Grandma, you have mad skillz at the *Price Is Right* game, and I'm really proud of you. But you should really try to get out of the house more often."

Grandma just smiled and said her life is exciting now that she's taking hip-hop dance lessons at the senior rec center. And her dance teacher, Krump Daddy, is "dope!"

Then she asked me if I wanted to see her "bust a move."

She was actually pretty good for a seventy-six-year-old! Grandma's a little WACKY, but you gotta LOVE her!

MONDAY, SEPTEMBER 9

This morning the halls were plastered with colorful posters for Random Acts of Avant-Garde Art, our annual school art show.

I'm SUPERexcited because the first prize for each class is $500, cash! SWEET!

That would be enough for me to buy a cell phone, a new outfit from the mall, AND art supplies.

But most important, winning that award could transform me from a "socially challenged ART DORK" to a "socially charmed ART DIVA" practically overnight!

Who woulda thunk my art skillz could get me into the CCP clique?!

So I rushed down to the school office to get an entry form and was surprised to see a line had already formed.

And guess who else was there picking one up?

MacKenzie ☹ !!!!

And as usual she was blabbering nonstop: "Like, since
I'm going to be a model/fashion designer/pop star, I
already have a portfolio of seven very HOT fashion
illustrations for my FAB-4-EVER clothing line,
which I also plan to wear on my very successful world
tour as the opening act for Miley Cyrus, who of
course will fall head over heels in love with MY designs
and buy like a million dollars' worth. Then I'm going
to enroll at a prestigious university like Harvard, Yale,
or the Westchester Fashion Institute of Cosmetology,
which, BTW, is owned by my aunt Clarissa!"

Okay. I'll admit I FREAKED OUT about having to
compete against MacKenzie.

She just kept staring at me with her icy blue eyes,
and my stomach felt queasy and I got chill bumps.

Then, suddenly, I had an epiphany and I TOTALLY
understood what my grandma meant when she said,

"You can be a CHICKEN
or a CHAMPION.
The choice is yours."

So I gathered all my strength and determination, took a deep breath, and mustered the courage to decide right there on the spot which one I was:

A BIG FAT CHICKEN!

When the office assistant asked if I was there to pick up an entry form for the avant-garde art show, I just froze and started clucking like a hen:

Buk, buk, buk-ka-a-ah!

Then, MacKenzie laughed, like ME entering the competition was the most ridiculous thing she had ever heard.

That's when I spotted the yellow sign-up sheet for

library shelving assistants, also known as LSAs. Every day during study hall, a few kids get excused to go to the school library to shelve books. An LSA's life is about as exciting as watching paint dry.

So, instead of trying to achieve my dream of winning a major art competition, I very STUPIDLY signed up to shelve DUSTY and BORING LIBRARY BOOKS!

MY FUTURE MISERABLE LIFE AS A LIBRARY SHELVING ASSISTANT

"IF I SEE ANOTHER BOOK, I'M GOING TO PUKE!"

And it's ALL MacKenzie's fault!! ☹

When I reported to the library during study hall, the librarian, Mrs. Peach, gave me a tour. She told me I would be working with two other girls who had signed up last week.

But what I wanted to know was WHO in their right mind would sign up to shelve library books as an EXTRACURRICULAR ACTIVITY?!

At least I had a good excuse.

I did it while I was temporarily INSANE from MacKenzie's icy stare, which had frozen my brain cells, slowed my heartbeat, and totally immobilized my body so I couldn't sign up for the avant-garde art competition.

I had the most horrible accident in French class today. While I was taking my French textbook out of my backpack, my perfumed body spray, called Sassy Sasha, fell on the floor.

Unfortunately, the little white nozzle thingy popped off, and it just kept spraying and spraying until the entire can was empty.

My teacher, Mr. Somethin' or Other (I can't pronounce his name because it sounds like a sneeze), started yelling a lot of stuff in French that sounded to me an awful lot like cuss words.

Then he evacuated all the students from the classroom because everyone was coughing and choking and their eyes were watering really bad.

And while we were standing in the hallway, waiting for the smell to go away, he asked me very rudely in English (which I DO understand) if I was trying to KILL him.

Okay! First of all, I don't like French class that much anyway. And second of all, it was JUST an accident!

I mean, it's NOT like my perfume was REALLY going to kill him. At least, I don't *think* so.

But, then again, WHAT if it actually DID?! What if my French teacher collapsed in the teachers' lounge while eating a corn dog at lunch and died from extreme Sassy Sasha asphyxiation??!!

And what if, for three whole days, no one noticed the foul odor coming from his dead body, since the

←STINK FUMES

school lunches normally smell a lot like rotting flesh?!

The police would launch an investigation, and I would be the main suspect.

Then the *CSI: Miami* crime-scene experts would conduct scientific tests on my French teacher's nose hairs and find traces of Sassy Sasha.

They would figure out that I was guilty of fumigating him with a lethal dose of my body spray.

And then, what if the CSI team SECRETLY planted ALL of the physical evidence on . . . MOI??!

(BTW, MOI is French for "ME"!)

I'd end up getting the ELECTRIC CHAIR during my freshman year, which would really SUCK!

And then afterward, I'd be like TOTALLY peeved because I missed drivers' ed class *and* my senior prom!

You gotta believe me,
I'm totally innocent!

I have nothing to hide.
Search my bedroom!

OMG! A DEAD BODY! How did HE get in here?!

Now that I think about it, Mr. Somethin' or
Other just LOVES MacKenzie, because she's really
good at French and she can pronounce his weird
sneeze-sounding name.

I bet if she had dropped HER Sassy Sasha body spray in his classroom and the nozzle thingy popped off, he would NOT have yelled at her or accused her of trying to kill him.

But that's because MacKenzie is

MISS PERFECT!!

I bet she's even going to WIN the avant-garde art competition!

And afterward, just out of spite, she'll probably check out like 189 books from the school library and then return them all the next day.

Of course, I'LL be the one STUCK having to put each and every one of them away, since I'm a STUPID library shelving assistant!

My pathetic life is SO UNFAIR, it makes me want to

SCREAM! ☹!!

WEDNESDAY, SEPTEMBER 11

Today everyone in the cafeteria was superexcited because MacKenzie was handing out invitations to her big birthday bash. The way Lisa Wang and Sarah Grossman were crying and hugging on each other, you would think they were gonna be on *My Super Sweet 16* or something. It was beyond DISGUSTING!

MacKenzie's PHONY friends crying PHONY tears and giving each other PHONY smiles and PHONY hugs!!

LISA WANG

SARAH GROSSMAN

They reminded me of the Olsen twins. For the life of me, I never understood why those sisters were always hugging on each other. They were the first set of non–Siamese twins who people actually thought were joined at the hip.

For the rest of the day, everyone MacKenzie invited to her party sucked up to her like a human vacuum cleaner. Except for **Brandon Roberts.**

When she gave him an invitation, she tried to flirt with him by twirling her hair around her finger and smiling really big. She even "accidentally" dropped her purse so he would pick it up for her, just like Tyra says to do when you're trying to get a guy to notice you.

But Brandon just glanced at MacKenzie's invitation, shoved it into his backpack, and walked right past her.

And, boy, did she get upset when he blew her off like that.

Then, a bunch of jocks trampled all over her new $300 Vera Bradley bag before she could pick it up off the floor. Personally, I kind of liked the dirty footprints better than that boring floral pattern.

Anyway, Brandon is SOOOO COOOOL!!!

From what I can tell, he seems to be kind of the quiet rebel type.

He's a reporter and photographer for the school newspaper and has won a few awards for his photojournalism.

Once he actually sat at my lunch table, but I don't think he noticed me staring at him.

Probably because his shaggy, wavy hair is FOREVER falling into his eyes.

And today in biology, when he asked if he could take a picture for the school newspaper of ME dissecting my frog, I almost DIED!!

I was shaking so badly, I could hardly hold the scalpel.

And now every tiny detail of his perfect face is permanently etched in my mind.

IS IT POSSIBLE THAT I AM FALLING IN LOVE FOR THE FIRST TIME?!

THE BIOLOGY OF MY HEARTBREAK
By Nikki Maxwell

I see you in my dreams
in your favorite white
button-down shirt,
sitting across from me
in the cafeteria.
I've never seen anyone
eat fries so beautifully.

I see you in biology class,
taking pictures for
the school newspaper, when
you whisper to the depths of my soul,
"Hold the frog at an angle."

For it is only you
who can make a photo
of a dissected frog
seem so vibrant.
So alive. Yet dead.

It hurts to feel this way,
to know that you'll never know me.
To want to run my fingers
through your dark, wavy hair,
as I realize that
the putrid smell of formaldehyde
and the dull gaze of a lifeless frog
will forever remind ME of US!

THURSDAY, SEPTEMBER 12

During my gym class, even the Scared-of-Balls girls were gossiping about MacKenzie's party. Like one of them would ever get invited.

They're the really prissy girls who hang in small groups and scream hysterically whenever a ball comes near them.

It could be a basketball, football, baseball, soccer ball, tennis ball, volleyball, beach ball, Ping-Pong ball, mothball, or even a meatball. They're NOT very picky.

SCARED-OF-BALLS GIRLS PLAY VOLLEYBALL

CHLOE and ZOEY

CHLOE and ZOEY freak out!

Red team WINS by 1 point!
Your grade is A+.
LOSERS, hit the showers!
Your grade is C.

Gym → Teacher

Our team loses ☹!

YEP! You can always count on the Scared-of-Balls girls to screw things up and lose the game for you.

It really sucks to have girls like Chloe and Zoey on your team. Especially if you absolutely HATE taking showers after gym class (just the thought of showering at school makes me nauseous).

It will totally be THEIR fault if I catch some kind of incurable disease from the slimy mold and mildew growing in those NASTY showers.

WHY I HATE SHOWERING IN GYM CLASS!

Me → BEFORE showering . . . slightly sweaty but clean & fresh!

Me ← AFTER showering . . . completely covered in stank, mildew, & slime!

63

I was really surprised when Chloe and Zoey came up to me after gym class and started talking. Of course, I pretended like I was NOT teed off at them for running away from the ball and making me have to take a shower.

Apparently, our librarian, Mrs. Peach, told them I was assigned to work with them in the library and they were actually EXCITED about it.

Like WHAT is so exciting about shelving library books??!!

But I just played along and pretended to be as thrilled about it as they were.

I was like, "OMG! OMG! I can't believe we're going to be shelving books together. How COOL is that?!"

We ended up eating lunch together at table 9, and it was really nice NOT having to eat alone for once.

Chloe's full name is Chloe Christina Garcia, and her family owns a software company. It was amazing because she has read like ALL of the latest novels.

She says she lives "vicariously" through the characters' joys and heartbreaks and learns a lot of stuff about life, love, boys, and kissing, which she plans to use when she goes to high school next year.

She said she owns 983 books and has read most of them twice.

I was like, "WOW!"

Zoey's full name is Zoeysha Ebony Franklin, and her mom is an attorney and her dad is a record company executive. She has met practically ALL of the biggest pop stars.

Zoey says she likes reading self-help and is currently seeking ways to "enhance" her relationship with the three "mother figures" in her life. She has a mom, a grandmother who helped raise her, and a stepmother.

I was really sympathetic, since I know from personal experience that having only ONE "mother figure" in your life can be traumatic and psychologically damaging.

Can you imagine having THREE?! OMG!

Then Zoey said, "How can you stand having a locker next to MacKenzie's? She is like so STUPID, she rubs lipstick on her forehead to make up her mind! And being really shallow can sometimes create multifaceted self-esteem issues."

I could NOT believe Zoey actually said that. I thought everyone at this school worshipped MacKenzie.

We laughed so hard that chewed-up carrot bits shot right out of my nose!

66

All three of us were like, EWWW! GROSS!

Then Chloe snickered, "Hey! Carrot-flavored boogers! Let's give them to MacKenzie so she can sprinkle them over her tofu salad as a low-carb topping. In the Clique series, those girls are forever doing evil stuff like that to their frenemies."

We laughed so loud at Chloe's joke that the kids sitting at tables 6 and 8 started staring at us.

I even saw MacKenzie glance our way. But then she looked away really fast so we wouldn't make the huge mistake of believing she actually acknowledged our existence. I could tell she was wondering what was going on.

So now I'm thinking about forgiving Chloe and Zoey for that whole shower FIASCO in gym class. I actually had a pretty good day today!

!!

I was pretty SICK and TIRED of hearing about MacKenzie and her STUPID little party! But since she is in my geometry class and I sit right behind her, I knew I was just going to have to suck it up and deal with it. I was trying my best to ignore her when she turned around, smiled at me, and did the STRANGEST thing!

She handed ME a bright pink invitation tied with a big white satin bow!

I gasped and almost fell out of my chair.

My brain was like

OMG! OMG! OMG!

It was the most beautiful thing I had ever seen, other than maybe that new iPhone I want.

Who would have thought that I would get an invitation to THE party of the year?!

Then it dawned on me that this might be some kind of really cruel JOKE.

I looked around the room for a hidden camera, half expecting Ashton Kutcher (I can't believe he's married to a woman older than my mom) to jump out of the closet and yell . . .

You just got PUNKED!!

Then I realized that most of the other girls in my class were staring at me with envy and disbelief.

It was really weird, because suddenly I noticed I had tiny lint balls all over my favorite hoodie.

And it made me feel self-conscious, so I tried to pick a few of them off.

None of MacKenzie's friends would be caught dead in a not-from-the-mall hoodie with lint balls on it.

So I made a mental note . . .

BURN CURRENT WARDROBE!

Worn-Out Sketchers

Low-Rise Jeans with Saggy Butt

Sweatshirt

Rest of My Embarrassing Wardrobe

Not-from-the-Mall Linty Hoodie

Scarf Knitted by Aunt

Belt

Birthday Present from Grandma

Baggy Tank Top

Dirty Gym Sock

Out-of-Style Clogs

MacKenzie was still smiling at me like I was her new BFF or something.

"Hey, hon! I was just wondering if you would—?"

But I was SO excited, I jumped right in before she could even finish her sentence.

"MacKenzie, I would LOVE to!" I gushed. "Thanks for asking me . . . hon!"

Okay. So I actually called her "hon," even though I always thought that word sounded superphony.

And yes, I was totally GEEKED and as HAPPY as Vanessa Anne Hudgens when she found out she was NOT getting kicked off *High School Musical 3!*

But mostly I was in SHOCK. I could hardly believe I was actually going to MacKenzie's party! Soon I was going to have really cool friends and a social life. And maybe even highlights, a pierced belly button, and a boyfriend.

I was starting to believe my *That's So Hot!* magazine was right. Maybe the key to happiness really was friends, fun, fashion, and flirting!!

ME, floating on air amid sunshine, rainbows, twinkling stars, and pink cotton-candy clouds, passionately clutching my invitation to MacKenzie's party over my heart!!

My hands were shaking as I untied the ribbon and tore open the envelope.

Suddenly, MacKenzie narrowed her eyes at me and scowled like I was something smeared on the bottom of her shoe.

"You IDIOT!" she hissed. "WHAT are you doing?!"

"Umm, opening m—my invitation?" I stammered.

I was already starting to have a really bad feeling about this whole party thing.

"Like I would invite you?!" She sneered, flipping her blond tresses and batting her long lashes at me in disgust. "Aren't you the new girl who hangs around my locker all the time like some kind of creepy stalker?"

"Well, yes . . . I mean, NO! Actually, my locker is right next to yours," I muttered.

"Are you sure?" she said, looking me up and down like I was lying to her or something. I couldn't believe she was actually pretending like she didn't know me. I've only had a locker next to hers like FOREVER!

"I'm VERY sure!" I said.

Then MacKenzie took out her Krazy Kissalicious lip gloss and applied like three extra-thick layers. After gazing at herself in her little compact mirror for two whole minutes (she is SO STUCK on herself!), she snapped it shut and glared at me.

"Before you so RUDELY interrupted me, I was simply asking if you would PASS my invitation to JESSICA! How was I supposed to know you were going to rip it open like some uncivilized GORILLA?" Mackenzie spat.

ME?!

Then everyone in the class turned around and stared at me.

I could NOT believe my ears! How dare that girl

actually call me UNCIVILIZED!!

"Oh. Okay. MY BAD!" I said, trying to sound coolly nonchalant about the whole thing while blinking back tears. "Um, who's Jessica?"

Suddenly I felt a sharp tap on my shoulder.

I turned around to face the girl sitting in the desk behind me.

She had long blond hair and was wearing pink, glittery lip gloss, a pink sweater, a pink miniskirt, and a headband trimmed with fake pink diamonds.

If I had spotted her in Toys "R" Us, I swear I would have probably mistaken her for a new fashion doll:

Pretty Ticked Jessica

I'M REALLY TICKED!

↑ "TOTALLY TICKED-OFF" JESSICA

"I'm Jessica," she announced, rolling her eyes at me. "I can't believe you opened MY invitation!"

I was desperately trying to tie the satin ribbon back on when she snatched the invitation from my hand so violently, I almost got a paper cut.

I felt like a TOTAL DORK! And, to make matters worse, I heard a few of the kids around me snickering.

This was absolutely THE most EMBARRASSING moment of my PATHETIC little life!!

And I had no doubt that, in just a matter of minutes, everyone in the ENTIRE school was going to be text-messaging gossip about me.

I was relieved when our math teacher, Mrs. Sprague, finally started class.

She spent the entire hour at the board reviewing how to calculate the volume of a cylinder, sphere, and cone for our upcoming test.

HOW TO CALCULATE VOLUME

THE VOLUME OF A CYLINDER
EQUALS THE (AREA OF THE BASE)
$\times$ HEIGHT = $\pi r^2 h$

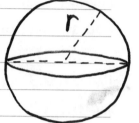

THE VOLUME OF A SPHERE = $4/3 \pi r^3$

THE VOLUME OF A CONE IS 1/3
THE (AREA OF BASE) $\times$ HEIGHT
= $1/3 \pi r^2 h$

But I was too freaked out to concentrate on math
formulas and was totally NOT listening. I just sat
there staring at the back of MacKenzie's head,
wishing I could disappear.

I guess I must have been really upset, because a tear
rolled down my cheek and splattered my geometry
notebook.

But I wiped it up with the sleeve of my not-from-the-mall, lint-ball-covered hoodie before anyone saw it.

Even though I was totally bummed about all the DRAMA over the invitation, I really wasn't that mad at MacKenzie.

I'M SUCH A LOSER!! If I was having a party, I WOULDN'T invite myself either!

It's a Party!

and You're NOT Invited!

SATURDAY, SEPTEMBER 14

I've had the most HORRIBLE week ever! WHY?

Because MacKenzie has been TRASHING my life:

1st She RUINED my chances in the avant-garde art competition.

2nd She DISSED me by NOT inviting me to her party.

3rd She RIDICULED me by calling me uncivilized.

4th She PUBLICLY HUMILIATED me by giving me an invitation and then UNINVITING me.

5th She tried to STEAL the one true love of my life, Brandon Roberts, by twirling her hair and flirting with him.

I planned to spend my ENTIRE weekend just sitting on my bed in my pajamas, STARING at the wall and SULKING.

Which, strangely enough,
always seems to make
me feel a lot better.

Me getting
my sulk on!

But my plans
were completely RUINED!

Around noon my mom came bouncing into my room
all cheerful and announced that for lunch we were
having a family cookout on the grill.

She said, "Honey, get dressed quick and come out
into the backyard and join the FUN!"

Well, obviously, I wasn't in the mood for "fun," and I
just wanted to be left alone.

And I didn't like hanging out in our backyard, because I have seen some fairly large spiders out there.

I have a thing about spiders—they creep me out.

Also, my physician has diagnosed me as being highly allergic to pests that suck human blood, such as spiders, mosquitoes, leeches, and vampires.

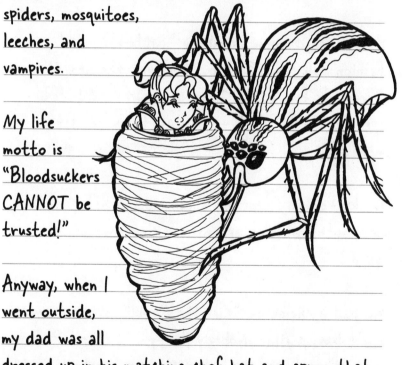

My life motto is "Bloodsuckers CANNOT be trusted!"

Anyway, when I went outside, my dad was all dressed up in his matching chef hat and apron that we got him for Father's Day.

It said "My Dad Is the World's Greatest Cook!" but most of the letters had faded off in the wash and it now says "My Dad eat s ook!"

How we got that gift was actually kind of embarrassing. Mom drove me and Brianna to Wal-Mart and gave us $30 to spend on a nice Father's Day present for Dad.

But after Brianna bought a "Tattoo-N-Tan" fashion doll for $9.99 and I bought the new Miley Cyrus CD for $14.00, we only had $6.01 left over to use for Dad, which wasn't a whole lot of money.

Lucky for us, I spotted these hideous hot pink chef hats with matching aprons in a clearance bin for only $3.87.

We had a choice of "Kiss the Cook!" "When Mamma Ain't Happy, Ain't Nobody Happy!" "Detroit Pistons RULE!" or "My Dad Is the World's Greatest Cook!" in orange fluorescent lettering.

And since the gift was dirt cheap, we still had like $2.14 left to buy a Father's Day card.

But I convinced Brianna that Dad would much rather have a handmade card from us that SHE could make for FREE using notebook paper, crayons, and glitter.

She totally bought into it, and I used the last few dollars to buy myself popcorn and an extra-large strawberry-mango smoothie. The snacks tasted good, considering the fact I was starving at the time and they came from a Wal-Mart.

Who woulda thunk Dad would have loved that tacky gift so much!

"This is the absolute BEST Father's Day gift I've ever received in my entire life!" he said, and got all teary-eyed.

Which is NOT saying much, because every year Brianna and I outdid ourselves finding CRUDDY Father's Day gifts.

But we always managed to snag some really great swag for ourselves. Father's Day is now our favorite holiday after our birthdays and Christmas.

Anyway, my dad was grilling the meat while whistling old disco tunes.

Then, out of the blue, he suddenly developed a major complication. Not with his whistling but his grilling.

I guess you could call it a bug problem.

So when he told me to run into the house and get the can of bug spray, I had a really BAD feeling about it.

I was like, "Dad, are you sure?"

And he was like, "I don't plan on sharing my twenty-dollar steaks with these pesky flies."

Well, THAT was a big mistake, because the bugs were NOT pesky flies.

BUG SPRAY

ZAP!

Roach & Ant Killer

NET WT 14 FL OZ

OUR FAMILY BARBECUE PICNIC
(A STORY IN PICTURES)

THE END

You'd think an experienced exterminator would recognize a fly when he saw one.

Unfortunately for Dad, he was dealing with a nest of very ANGRY HORNET WASPS!!

Well, our cookout ended up being a total disaster!

To make Dad feel better, we all complimented him on how handsome he looked in his snazzy chef hat and apron, even though he was a little dirty from knocking over the neighbor lady's garbage cans when he was running away from those wasps.

POOR DAD ☹!!

However, the good news is that I was able to go back up to my room and put in a few more hours of intense sulking. WOO HOO!

Today we had our math test on calculating volume, and I was really nervous. Mainly because I am not that good at math.

The last time I got a decent grade in this subject was way back in first grade. And even then I almost got half the problems wrong.

It just so happened that I sat across from Andrea Snarkowski, the smartest girl in the entire first grade. We were taking a test on addition when I kind of "accidentally" noticed that Andrea's answer to one of the problems was different from mine. So, at the last minute, I decided to cross out my answer with an X and use the one she had come up with.

It was a good thing I did so, because I got an A on the test! My teacher was so pleased with my miraculous improvement—on a good day I usually did D+ work—she gave me a smiley face gold star. And only geniuses like Andrea Snarkowski earned smiley face gold stars.

Since I had morphed into a brilliant math scholar,
I also won the class Student of the Month Award,
and my picture appeared in our community newspaper.

NIKKI → MAXWELL

Me in first grade, with a perfect score on my math test after Andrea Snarkowski kind of helped me out a little bit

Math   Crystal
1   2
+1 +2
2   4
Good Job!

STUDENT OF THE MONTH

My mom and dad were SO proud of me!

They made 127 copies of my newspaper article and
mailed them out to every single one of my relatives
all across the nation.

I can only imagine how happy and excited they

were for me when they opened their letters:

← MY THIRD COUSIN BILLY-BOB

"Ethel, call the cops! We just got another letter from that crazy stalker!!"

Okay, so maybe some of my relatives didn't recognize me right away.

But if they *had*, I'm pretty sure they would have been really proud.

Anyway, my geometry test on calculating volume was really hard.

I know I should have studied more. But since I spent the entire weekend sulking, it kind of cut into my study time.

I pretty much just prayed like crazy through the whole test.

Sometimes even out loud:

"PLEASE, PLEASE, PLEASE HELP ME TO PASS THIS TEST! I'M REALLY SORRY ABOUT SNOOZING IN CHURCH LAST SUNDAY AND IT WON'T HAPPEN AGAIN. ALSO, CAN YOU TELL ME IF THE FORMULA FOR THE VOLUME OF A CYLINDER IS $\pi r^2 h$ OR $\pi h r^2$? AND, WHEN YOU CALCULATE A SPHERE, DO YOU MULTIPLY THE . . . ?"

I guess a few people sitting near me must have overheard.

I was TOO happy when that test was *finally over!*

As I was putting my stuff into my backpack to go

to my next class, I couldn't help noticing MacKenzie eyeballing me all evil-like.

Then she walked up to Jessica and said, "Today is the last day to enter the avant-garde art competition, and I have to take my entry form down to the office. I'll meet you at my locker. Okay, hon?"

Then Jessica stared at me and said really loud, "Mac, I just KNOW you're going to win first place. Your fashion illustrations are SO um . . . BOOTYLICIOUS!"

I could NOT believe Jessica said that, because "bootylicious" is like so yesterday!

But the thing that really freaked me out was when MacKenzie smirked at me and was all like, "Nikki, everyone in the entire school knows you're too CHICKEN to enter the art competition because I'M a better artist than you are. So don't bother!"

Okay. Even though MacKenzie didn't actually SAY those words to me, she definitely looked like she was THINKING them.

And, either way, it was a humongous INSULT to my integrity.

Then she flipped her hair and sashayed out of the classroom. I just HATE it when MacKenzie sashays!

How DARE she talk about the art competition right to my face like that??!!

Especially when it was HER fault I DIDN'T enter to begin with.

This whole situation just TICKED me off!

Suddenly, I just totally lost it and screamed at the top of my lungs, "MacKenzie STARTED this WAR, and now I'M going to FINISH it!!"

But I said it in my head, so no one else heard it but me.

Then I made a solemn promise to myself:

I, NIKKI J. MAXWELL,
being of sound mind and body,
am officially entering the
AVANT-GARDE ART
COMPETITION!!

I was going to show MacKenzie once and for all that I had MAD art skillz. And MINE were WAY MADDER than HERS!

So I grabbed all my stuff and marched right down to the office to fill out an entry form.

Sure enough, MacKenzie was still in there, applying

her fourteenth layer of lip gloss and bragging
nonstop about her fashion illustrations.

". . . and everyone thinks my original designs are so
HAWT, and I'm going to be RICH and FAMOUS and
move to HOLLYWOOD and blah-blah, blah-blah,
blah-blah, blah!"

I was just casually chilling out behind a big plotted
plant right outside the office door, minding my own
business, when, *finally,* MacKenzie left.

But it was NOT like
I was spying on her
or anything.

I just didn't
want to attract
a lot of
attention to
myself or have
MacKenzie think I was
making a big deal out of
the fact that I was entering the competition.

Although, to be honest, it WAS a big deal.

It was THE most important thing I had EVER attempted in my entire fourteen years of life here on planet Earth.

I rushed into the office and quickly filled out an entry form.

As I handed it to the assistant, I felt a rush of panic, excitement, and nausea, all mixed up together whirling around in my stomach like leftovers in a garbage disposal.

I walked out of the office and collapsed against the wall.

My heart was pounding so hard, I could hear it in my ears. I began to wonder if this whole thing was a big mistake.

Then, out of the blue, I got a really creepy feeling that someone was watching me, even though the halls seemed empty.

Suddenly, a leaf on the plant I had hid behind moved, and I saw this EYE staring out at me! Then two eyes. Very icy blue ones.

MacKenzie (YES, *the* MacKenzie) was peeping out at me from behind that big potted plant near the office door!

SHE WAS LIKE, SO BUSTED!

Finally, MacKenzie climbed out of the plant and sashayed over to the drinking fountain like she was thirsty or something. But it was very obvious to me that she was just trying to use WATER TORTURE to FORCE me to change my mind about entering the art competition.

"OOPSY! MY BAD!"

MacKenzie tried to act all innocent and apologetic, like the whole squirting me with water thing was just an accident. But I looked into her beady little eyes and could tell she absolutely meant to do it.

I still could not get over the fact that I had actually caught her SPYING on me!

Which kind of made me ANGRY, because I don't follow her around, SPYING on her and getting all up in her Kool-Aid (which, BTW, means "business").

Well, at least not that often.

Today was like *TOTALLY* an exception, mainly because we were both turning in entries for the art competition at the same time.

But to stoop so low as to SPY on me?!

THAT GIRL IS
ONE *SICK*
LITTLE PUPPY!

I can't believe I'm actually writing this while hiding in the janitor supply closet!! I know it's supergrungy in here and smells like an old, wet, mildewy mop, but I didn't know where else to go. I ABSOLUTELY

HATE! HATE! HATE! HATE! HATE! HATE! HATE! HATE! HATE! HATE! HATE! HATE!

THIS STUPID SCHOOL!!

Today at lunch, I was carrying my tray and trying to get to table 9, where I was supposed to meet Chloe and Zoey. Things were going pretty good, because I had managed to sneak past the jock table without the football players making those embarrassing farting noises with their armpits.

But as I was walking past MacKenzie's table, I really wasn't paying attention. She and Jessica must have STILL been pretty mad at me about the party invitation and the art competition, because this is what happened:

ME IN THE LUNCHROOM TRYING TO GET TO TABLE 9

I tripped, and suddenly, everything started moving in slow motion. My lunch tray went flying up over my head, and I heard a very familiar voice shrieking,

"Noooooooo!"

Then in HORROR, I realized it was MINE!

I fell flat on the floor and was so stunned, I could barely breathe. My spaghetti and cherry jubilee dessert were smeared across my face and the front of my clothes. I looked like a life-size version of one of Brianna's messy finger paintings.

I just closed my eyes and lay there like a beached whale, with every inch of my body aching. Even my hair hurt. However, the worst part was that the entire cafeteria was laughing like crazy.

I was SO embarrassed, I wanted to DIE. I could barely see, because I had cherry jubilee in my eyes and it made everything look red and really blurry.

Finally, I gathered the strength to crawl to my knees.

But each time I tried to get up, I slipped in the mixture of spaghetti and milk and fell back down again.

I have to admit, I probably looked hilarious sloshing around in my lunch like that.

And if it hadn't actually been happening to ME, I definitely would have been laughing my butt off along with everyone else.

Then, MacKenzie folded her arms, glared at me, and yelled,

"SO, NIKKI, ARE YOU HAVING A NICE TRIP?!"

Of course, that witty little comment made everyone laugh even harder.

It was the CRUELEST thing MacKenzie could have possibly said, especially since she was partially responsible for my "trip."

I was so humiliated, I started to cry.

The good news was the tears washed all the gunk out of my eyes, and I could see again.

But the bad news was, all I could see was this guy kneeling over me with a camera dangling in my face.

And only ONE person in the whole entire school owns a camera like that.

In a split second, I knew *exactly* what was going to appear on the FRONT PAGE of the next issue of our school newspaper ☹!

And I was NOT going to be sending *that* article to any of my relatives.

It was very clear to me that some way, somehow, MacKenzie had completely charmed Brandon with her awesome beautyliciousness and lured him over to the DARK SIDE!

And then BRAINWASHED him!

How could my CRUSH—the secret LOVE of my life—do such a HORRIBLE and WICKED thing to me?!

I felt like I had been stabbed in the heart with my favorite lucky ink pen—the hot pink sparkly one with the feathers, beads, and sequins on the end—and left to die. On the floor of the cafeteria. With everyone watching. And laughing. By my beloved BRANDON!!

Then the most bizarre thing happened!

Brandon kind of smiled at me, slid his camera out of the way, grabbed my hand, and pulled me up off the floor.

"You . . . okay?"

I tried to say, "Yes," but my voice just made a gurgling sound like I was strangling or something. I swallowed and took a deep breath.

"Sure. I'm okay. I had spaghetti for dinner yesterday but it wasn't nearly this slippery!"

I cringed. I couldn't believe I just said that. I am such a DORK!!

Then I watched, spellbound, as Brandon handed me

a napkin in what seemed like slow motion. I almost DIED, right there on the spot, when our fingers accidentally TOUCHED . . .

. . . ever so slightly, like a gentle but wild squirrel slurping sweet nectar from one of those dainty purpley flowers in my mother's garden that my dad accidentally sprayed with weed killer. Our eyes locked and for a split second it was as if we were gazing into the deep, misty cavern of each other's wounded souls. I will FOREVER remember the words he whispered into my trembling ear:

"Um . . . I think you have . . . something on your face?"

I blushed and my knees started feeling all wobbly. "Probably my lunch . . ."

"Yeah, probably . . ."

Unfortunately, our very serious emo convo (which, BTW, means "emotional conversation") was rudely interrupted by Mr. Snodgrass, our lunchroom monitor. But everyone calls him Mr. Snot and a not-so-nice word.

He started cleaning up the mess on the floor and lecturing me about my responsibility as a young adult to keep my food on my tray at all times. Brandon rolled his eyes at Mr. Snodgrass in a very chivalrous manner, and then he kind of smiled at me again.

"I guess I'll see you in biology."

"Yeah . . . okay. And thanks. You know, for the napkin."

"Hey, no prob."

"Actually, we have napkins just like this at home.

My mom got them on sale. At Wal-Mart . . ."

"Oh, that's, um . . . cool. Well, later."

"Sure, see ya, in bio."

Then Brandon picked up his backpack and left the cafeteria.

I just clutched the napkin over my heart and sighed.

In spite of everything that had just happened, I suddenly felt VERY happy and butterflyish all over.

But that feeling lasted only about ten seconds, because that's how long it took me to notice MacKenzie.

→ MACKENZIE

She was SO angry, her whole face was all droopy and distorted.

She actually looked a little SCARY!

"I hope you're not STUPID enough to think HE'D like a LOSER like you?" she howled like a banshee.

But I guess I was still kind of disoriented, because I didn't have the slightest idea what she was talking about.

"Um . . . he, WHO?" I asked.

That's when Jessica blurted out, "You are such a KLUTZ. OMG! Look at her! I think she PEED her pants!"

And then MacKenzie was like, "OMG! You're right. She did PEE her pants!"

And both of them started laughing and pointing at me again.

I just rolled my eyes at them and said, "Yeah right! I spilled MILK on my pants. Don't you morons know milk when you see it?"

Then I ran out of the cafeteria and went straight to the nearest girls' restroom.

Inside, there were about five girls at the mirror trying out one another's lip gloss flavors.

They completely froze and just stared at me in horror with their mouths wide open.

It was like they had *NEVER* seen anyone covered from head to foot in spaghetti and cherry jubilee before.

Some people are so RUDE!

I kind of staggered back into the hallway like a zombie. But instead of leaving a trail of slimy, rotted flesh, I left a trail of spaghetti, sauce, and cherry jubilee.

Then I noticed the door of the janitor's utility closet near the drinking fountain was cracked open a little bit. I peeked inside, and since no one was in there, I snuck in and closed the door.

I felt so HORRIBLE! That's when I burst into tears and starting writing in my diary.

Pretty soon I heard some vaguely familiar voices whispering and snickering outside the door.

I just knew MacKenzie and her peeps were trying to track me down to harass me some more about peeing my pants.

"Are you sure she's in there?"

"I think so. The spaghetti leads right up to this

door and stops. And look, cherry jubilee footprints! She *has* to be in there."

I was like, JUST GREAT!

At that moment I would have given anything to just DISAPPEAR into thin air.

Then they actually had the nerve to knock on my door. Well, not exactly *my* door, but the door to the janitor's closet.

I felt like the victim in one of those horror movies where the girl is home alone and hears a knock at the front door.

And when she goes to open the door, everyone in the audience is yelling, "DON'T OPEN IT! DON'T OPEN IT!"

But she opens the door anyway because she doesn't *know* she's in a horror movie.

Who's that knocking?

Hey, maybe it's the pizza guy!

So . . . . you say you're giving out FREE haircuts?!

But I was NOT stupid!

I KNEW I was trapped in a horror flick, so I

DIDN'T open the door to the janitor's closet.
All of a sudden it got really quiet, and I suspected
it was a trick to make me think they had left.

But I had a feeling in my gut they were still out there.

"Nikki, are you okay?! We just heard what happened."

"Yeah, we wanted to make sure you were all right!"

That's when I finally recognized the voices.

It was CHLOE and ZOEY!!

Zoey said, "Girl, don't make me bust this door down,
because you know I will do it!"

That kind of made me laugh, because Zoey has trouble
opening her locker. And sometimes even her bottled water.

I was like, *Yeah, right!*

Then Chloe said, "If you're not going to come out
and talk to us, we're coming IN!"

The next thing I knew, Chloe and Zoey were poking their heads inside the janitor's closet and acting all goofy.

Chloe was snorting and giving me "jazz hands," and Zoey was sticking out her tongue and giving me the "stink eye."

They were like . . .

"WHAT'S UP, GIRLFRIEND!!"

For some reason, seeing them made me start crying all over again. Soon, the three of us were just chilling out in the janitor's closet talking about all the drama with Jessica and MacKenzie.

But I left out the part about Brandon on purpose, because I was still kind of embarrassed about it. Plus, I was pretty sure he'd pick MacKenzie over me any day. If I were a guy, I sure would. I was so NOT getting my hopes up about Brandon actually liking me.

Pretty soon the lunch period was almost over. Chloe and Zoey helped scrub most of the food stains off my clothes with paper towels and hand soap right at the big sink.

There were still some stains we couldn't get off, though. I couldn't believe it when Zoey ran to her locker to get me her favorite lucky sweater to wear to cover them up.

And Chloe said that if I applied an extra amount of her Candy Apple Swirl ultrashiny lip gloss along with her midnight blue eyeliner, everyone (especially the guys) would notice my beautiful luscious lips and dreamy eyes instead of the pee stain . . . er . . . I mean, MILK stain on the front of my pants.

Which, lucky for me, was not that noticeable, since it was starting to dry up.

In spite of how bad things went at lunch, I definitely feel a lot better now. I guess maybe I don't hate this school quite as much anymore. But I bet Brandon thinks I'm a

TOTAL KLUTZ!!

I think I'm suffering from Nocellphoneaphobia.

I know it sounds like some really nasty disease where you're covered from head to toe with itchy, runny sores, or something hideous like that.

But it's actually the irrational fear of *NOT* having a cell phone.

The worse thing about Nocellphoneaphobia is that it sometimes causes hallucinations and makes you do insanely STUPID things.

I think I had an attack of this very debilitating disease on my way home from school today.

I thought for sure I saw a tiny, cute cell phone thingy that clips around your ear lying on the sidewalk near our mailbox.

I was like, SWEET!! A FREE cell phone thingy! It's ALL GOOD!

But when I took a closer look, it was kind of a bright peachy color.

I guessed that what I had found was actually a HEARING AID.

Of course, I was devastated when I finally figured this out, because I was really pumped about having found a free cell phone thingy just lying there on the sidewalk.

I figured it probably belonged to Mrs. Wallabanger, the little old lady who lives next door.

I suspected she was hard of hearing because for the past few days, whenever I said "Good morning" to her on my way to school, she would ask me to repeat what I said like seven times.

She has a scrawny lil' Yorkie named Creampuff, and she walks him twice a day.

Creampuff looks like a fuzzy ball of lint on four legs, but he's as vicious as a Doberman.

Anyway, I spent five minutes trying to decide whether or not to knock on Mrs. Wallabanger's door and ask if she had lost her hearing aid. But I figured if she HADN'T, it would be a waste of my time and energy. And if she HAD, it would be an EVEN BIGGER waste of my time and energy. I was right. This is what happened:

ME
(Talking very loud)

MRS. WALLABANGER
(Not really hearing me)

GRRRRR!! GRRRRR!!

CREAMPUFF
(Growling and trying to bite me)

WHAT I SAID	WHAT SHE SAID
Hi, Mrs. Wallabanger. I just stopped by to ask if you lost your hearing aid?	What did you say, missy?
Your HEARING AID!! Is it lost?	Eh? Speak up, why don't cha?
Did you lose your HEARING AID?!	Eh? You say, I need to lose my HAIRY LEGS . . . ?!!
HEARING AID!! HEARING AID!!	Don't get fresh with me, you little whippersnapper!! My HAIRY LEGS are NONE of your BEESWAX. GET OFF MY PROPERTY!!

I was like, "Never mind!" My little chat with Mrs.
Wallabanger did NOT go well. So I figured I'd just
hold on to her hearing aid for a while. Since she only
comes out of her house to walk her dog, what's the
WORST that could happen?!

"Hey, lady! Be careful! Don't step in that big pile of . . . !"

"Didn't you hear me, ma'am? I said, watch out for the WET CEMENT!!"

"Creampuff, dear, is that sound the mating call of the yellow-bellied swamp goose?!"

Okay, so maybe the WORST that could happen is Mrs. Wallabanger gets run over by a semitruck!

But could you really say it was MY fault?!

Today, my social studies teacher, Mr. Simmons, reminded the class that our project on how recycling can help stop global warming is due on Monday. I didn't have the slightest idea what I was going to do. I figured I'd just wait until my creative juices started flowing and come up with something the night before, like I always do.

Anyway, at lunchtime, I saw a group of CCP girls crowded around MacKenzie raving about her brand-new Prada cell phone. And, get this! She had a cell phone thingy clipped on her ear that looked almost identical to the hearing aid I had found.

Even though I was starting to feel a little guilty about keeping Mrs. Wallabanger's hearing aid, I suddenly got this fantastically brilliant idea for my social studies project. My project was going to:

1. encourage recycling to cut down on pollution

2. help stop global warming by reducing the number

124

of "hot air bags" yakking nonstop on cell phones

3. boost my popularity at school by making everyone think I owned an expensive new cell phone thingy, just like MacKenzie's

I borrowed my dad's video camera and taped my project.

HOW TO MAKE A FAUX CELL PHONE THINGY FROM AN OLD HEARING AID
(A Social Studies Project by NIKKI MAXWELL)

Hi, I'm Nikki, and I'm going to show you how to make a faux cell phone thingy from an old hearing aid. The word "faux" is pronounced "pho," as in "phony." It's a French word snobby people use that means "fake" or "knockoff."

STEP ONE:
GATHER YOUR SUPPLIES

For this project you will need:

● 1 hearing aid
(recycled, found,
or "borrowed")
● 1 paper plate
● 1 can of spray
paint (black or
silver depending on
the model you plan
to make)

STEP TWO:
PAINT YOUR HEARING AID

Utilizing my
very expert and
highly creative
skills in arts and
crafts, I place
Mrs. Wallabang—I
mean, *MY* recycled
hearing aid on a
paper plate.

Then I carefully spray paint it a shiny, metallic black.

126

Next, I allow the paint to dry for thirty minutes.

Recycling is a vital step in stopping global warming, as my very fine teacher, Mr. Simmons, has taught our social studies class. [Waves to Mr. Simmons.]

STEP THREE:
MAKE UP A SCRIPT FOR YOUR FAUX CALLS

Even though your phone thingy will look so real it'll fool your family and friends, you must always keep in mind that it is NOT real. This means you will have to make up faux (phony) things to say while you are wearing it, like:

1. "Dee-dee-dee! Dee-dee-dee!"
(This is your phone ringing. I recommend using a very high-pitched voice for authenticity. Or you can sing or hum your favorite song for a Top 40 ring tone.)

2. "OMG! I CAN'T believe she actually said that! I'm going to hang up and call (insert the name of your biggest school gossip) right now!"

3. "I'd really love to give you my cell phone number, but I get SO many calls that my 'rents said I'm not allowed to give it out anymore or they'll take away my phone. But, if you like, I can put you on my waiting list to receive it . . ."

4. "Hello? Hello? Can you hear me now? You're breaking up! Hello?!"

5. "#@$%&!! Another dropped call! I HATE having (insert the name of a cruddy cell phone company) as a service provider!"

6. "Hello, I'd like to order a large pizza with extra (insert favorite pizza toppings) and hold the (insert least favorite pizza toppings). Thanks!"

7. "SHOOT! This stupid thing isn't working anymore! Either my battery is low or I need to buy some more minutes. Sorry!"

(The very convincing lie you tell when someone asks to borrow your cool phone to make a quick call. REMEMBER, IT'S *NOT REAL!*)

STEP FOUR:
CLIP YOUR FAUX CELL PHONE THINGY ON YOUR EAR AND START TALKING.

Congratulations!

Your new faux cell phone thingy is now ready for public use!

IMPRESS your family and AMAZE your friends.

But most important, do YOUR part to help STOP global warming by recycling an old hearing aid into a faux cell phone thingy today!

THE END

Unfortunately, I had a little complication with step four. After dinner I decided to practice humming my ring tone so I could start receiving faux calls in school tomorrow. I had been wearing my phone for only about five minutes when I felt a mild irritation and burning sensation on my right ear and the area around it.

However, after ten minutes, it turned into a full-blown rash. A really itchy, irritating one.

It didn't take long for me to come to the conclusion that the rash was all my MOM'S fault!

Why she never bothered to tell me I was highly allergic to shiny, metallic black spray paint, I'll never know. I mean, she HAD to have known this information. Right? This is the same woman who gave birth to me!

Lucky for me, my dad still had some antihistamine cream left over from the time he got attacked by those wasps. So I slathered it all over my ear and the side of my face.

Since I had no further use for Mrs. Wallabanger's hearing aid, I decided the moral and right thing to do was to return it to her.

ANONYMOUSLY!

I placed her hearing aid in a little box with a bow on it and attached a note. Then I put it on her front step, rang her doorbell, and ran away. It's not like I was scared of her or anything. I just kind of wanted it to be a surprise.

To:
Mrs.
Wallabanger ☺

Later that evening, I saw Mrs. Wallabanger walking her dog and, sure enough, she was wearing her hearing aid and a huge smile.

If I EVER find another hearing aid on the sidewalk, I'm definitely going to just leave it there. I only hope:

1. I get a decent grade on my global warming project and

2. This ugly rash goes away before school tomorrow

ICK! ☹!!

I was up and getting ready for school when I noticed I *STILL* had that rash from my faux cell phone! I almost choked on my minty-fresh, tartar control, extra-brightening, mouthwash-strength, cavity-fighting gel toothpaste.

Now that my crush, Brandon, had *finally* noticed I was alive, there was NO WAY I was going to school with a rash that made my ear look like it belonged to a severely sunburned Keebler Elf. You know, the ones who bake cookies inside a tree trunk infested with ants, termites, centipedes, and beetles. I always wondered what those brown crunchy things were in their cookies. Ewwww!

Anyway, I knew my mom was NOT going to let me stay home from school unless I was spiking a temperature of at least 289 degrees. Which, BTW, is the same temp she uses to bake her Thanksgiving turkey.

MOM'S TEMPERATURE REQUIREMENTS FOR A THANKSGIVING TURKEY AND A SICK DAUGHTER

←289°→

My mom's life motto is "Hey! Why let a little case of gangrene or leprosy get in the way of achieving a good education?!"

After trying every trick in the book, I *finally* figured out how to convince my mom I was too ill to go to school. I had to PRETEND to throw up all over myself.

Now, how SICK is THAT?!

I came up with this idea last spring after Brianna had the stomach flu. Mom took time off from work and let my little sister stay home from school for an entire week.

On top of that, she totally pampered Brianna by buying her all of her favorite Disney movies on DVD and a new computer game to keep her occupied while she was in bed.

I think all that vomiting must have really gotten to Mom. About three weeks later, I stayed home from school with a bad case of strep throat and was hoping to at least get a couple of new CDs out of it. But all Mom bought me was a cruddy box of Popsicles! And, to make matters worse, they were the really gross low–calorie kind with no sugar. They tasted like frozen pickle juice on a stick. I was like delish! ☹

Thanks a million, Mom!

But I have to admit, Brianna WAS a lot sicker than I was. She couldn't keep anything down, not even water!

I refused to go anywhere near her unless I was suited up in full "puke protection" gear:

↖ Me ready for Brianna's projectile vomiting due to her stomach flu. Yuck!

Since I was pretty sure Mom was not going to consider my rash serious enough to let me stay home from school, I decided to run downstairs and make a quick batch of phony vomit, aka, "faux puke." Which I needed because of the rash caused by my faux cell phone. It was just another one of life's surprising little ironies.

Lucky for me, I was the first one out of bed, which meant I had the kitchen completely to myself for about fifteen minutes. Since things were going to get a little messy, I changed into my old heart pj's and rushed downstairs.

My secret recipe was easy to make, and it looked and smelled like the real thing:

STAY-HOME-FROM-SCHOOL FAUX VOMIT

1 cup of cooked oatmeal

1/2 cup of sour cream (or buttermilk ranch dressing or anything that smells like rancid, sour milk)

2 chopped cheese sticks (for chunkiness)

1 uncooked egg (for authentic slimy texture)

1 can of split pea soup (for putrid green color)

1/4 cup of raisins (to increase gross-osity)

Mix ingredients and simmer over low heat for 2 minutes.

Let mixture cool to warm vomit temperature.
Use liberally as needed.
Makes 4 to 5 cups.

WARNING: This stuff is SO gross that it might really make you sick to your stomach and cause you to really throw up. In which case, you will really need to stay home from school ☹!

I poured about 2 cups into a bowl, ran back upstairs to my room, and dumped it down the front of my heart pj's. Then I yelled down the hall in a really whiney voice:

"MOM! Please come quick! I don't feel so good. My stomach is really queasy and I think I'm going to . . .

blecchuuarggh!"

Of course, it worked like a charm ☺!! Mom was totally convinced and said that not only did I have an upset stomach but also there was a mild rash on my ear.

She said that since I was not running a temperature, I'd probably feel better after a day of bed rest. I told her that suddenly I was feeling a lot better already (wink wink). Then she cleaned up my "mess," helped with my bubble bath, and tucked me back into bed with a kiss.

I actually slept until the Tyra Banks show came on at noon. I just LOVE that girl!

However, when I went into the kitchen to grab a bite for lunch, I suddenly realized I had totally FORGOTTEN to pour the leftovers of my faux vomit down the garbage disposal.

So when I saw that my mom had left a note for me on the counter right next to the now empty pot of puke, I just KNEW she was onto me and I was in really BIG trouble. I totally panicked and my stomach started feeling queasy, but this time FOR REAL! Her note said:

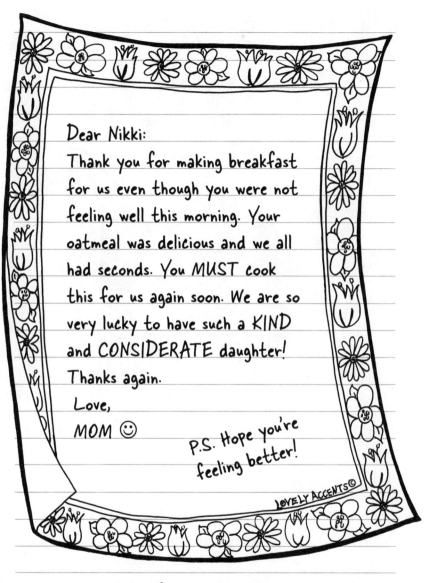

Dear Nikki:

Thank you for making breakfast for us even though you were not feeling well this morning. Your oatmeal was delicious and we all had seconds. You MUST cook this for us again soon. We are so very lucky to have such a KIND and CONSIDERATE daughter! Thanks again.

Love,
MOM ☺

P.S. Hope you're feeling better!

LOVELY ACCENTS©

I spent the entire afternoon just lounging around, watching television, and raiding the fridge. I even ordered a pizza!

ME GETTING
MY GRUB ON
☺!

Plus, I had THREE things to be VERY happy about:

1. The Tyra Banks show ROCKED!

2. My rash completely cleared up.

3. My parents think I'm a fourteen-year-old
Rachael Ray.

I think Chloe and Zoey have totally lost their minds!

First of all, they practically freaked out when Mrs. Peach announced she was taking six of her most hardworking and committed LSAs on a five-day field trip to the New York City Public Library to participate in National Library Week.

From what I understand, it's like a big Mardi Gras celebration for people obsessed with libraries. Mrs. Peach is already making plans, even though it's in April, which is still a whole seven months away.

But when Mrs. Peach said there was going to be a "Meet-n-Greet" with a lot of really famous authors like Kate Brian, Scott Westerfeld, D. J. MacHale, and some guy I've never heard of (Zoey said he was Dr. Phil's son and her FAVE self-help guru for teens), Chloe and Zoey actually started jumping up and down and screaming their heads off.

I was like, "Girlfriends, take a CHILL PILL, PUH-LEEZE!"

MRS. PEACH'S ANNOUNCEMENT . . .

I mean, I was excited, but not THAT excited. Now, if Mrs. Peach had announced she was taking us to NYC to have a "Meet-n-Greet" with like the Jonas Brothers, Kanye West, AND Justin Timberlake, I'd have hyperventilated, fainted, and rolled around on the floor having seizures.

WHAT I *WISH* MRS. PEACH HAD ANNOUNCED . . . !

Chloe and Zoey are really nice and sweet friends. But I have to admit that sometimes they are . . . like . . . SO WEIRD!!

The whole time we were shelving books, they were talking nonstop about how we needed to do something really special to convince Mrs. Peach to select the three of us for the trip to NYC.

"Well, why don't we just try to be the MOST hardworking and committed LSAs?" I suggested. "And we could start by maybe dusting off the books."

It was a no-brainer to me.

But Chloe and Zoey both looked at me like I was crazy.

"ALL of the other LSAs are going to be doing boring stuff like THAT to impress her!" Chloe groaned.

"Yeah! We need to come up with a secret plan that will blow Mrs. Peach's mind!" Zoey said excitedly.

Okay, so dusting the library books was NOT exactly a mind-blowing idea. But it definitely would have solved my little sneezing problem.

We were putting out a batch of brand-new magazines when Chloe swiped a *That's So Hot!* and buried her nose in it. Suddenly, she gasped and then shrieked:

"OMG! This is *exactly* what we should do!"

"What? Get makeovers and become teen supermodels?" I asked sarcastically.

"NO! Of course not!" Chloe said, rolling her eyes at me.

"I know! I know! Make. Your. Face. Zit. Proof!"

Zoey said, reading one of the captions printed on the magazine cover.

"No way!" Chloe said. "Not that!" She was so excited, her eyes were practically bulging out of their sockets. Then she shoved the magazine in our faces and pointed.

"... THIS!!"

Me and Zoey were like, "TATTOOS?! Are you NUTS?!"

"A tattoo promoting reading would be PERFECT! And it would show that we're serious and committed. Then Mrs. Peach will choose us for the field trip for sure!" Chloe squealed.

"That's a WICKED idea!" Zoey said, staring in awe at the beautiful, tattooed model in the magazine.

"I bet we're going to look as cool as her once we get ours! *SWEET!*"

Okay. I could deal with going on a boring field trip for National Library Week. But there was just no way I was getting a tattoo to *CELEBRATE* going on a boring field trip for National Library Week. I mean, *WHAT* kind of tattoo would I even get?

I had to think fast. "Um . . . I agree this is *the* coolest idea, you guys. But I just found out a few days ago that I'm . . . superallergic to . . . spray painted hearing aids."

Chloe and Zoey looked really confused.

"Why would anyone spray paint a hearing aid? That's like SO bizarre!" Chloe said, shaking her head like I was really pathetic. Zoey agreed.

That's when I lost it and yelled at them both, "You know what I think is BIZARRE? Bizarre is getting a TATTOO for National Library Week!!" But I just said that inside my head, so no one else heard it but me.

"Well, spray paint and tattoo ink are *both* kind of . . . um, colorful, so I'm pretty sure I'm allergic," I said. "Which is really unfair because I was totally looking forward to getting a tattoo one day before I die."

"Well, if it's a medical problem, we understand. Right, Zoey? Hey! Why don't you help us pick out our tattoos?" Chloe was trying to make me feel better.

"Yeah, we should ask our parents to take us to get them this weekend!" Zoey said excitedly. "I can hardly wait to see the look on Mrs. Peach's face when she sees our tattoos!"

But I already knew what her face was going to look like when she saw Chloe and Zoey . . .

POOR MRS. PEACH!! ☹

I was hoping Chloe and Zoey were over their wacky idea of getting tattoos for National Library Week. Thank goodness their parents said, "No way!" But when I saw them in gym class, they were still pretty upset.

Our gym teacher divided us up into groups of three for our ballet skills test, and at first, I was happy that me, Chloe, and Zoey were together. Each group was supposed to pick classical music from the teacher's CD collection and then make up a short dance routine using the five ballet positions we had learned over the past weeks. Since I knew all of them, I was sure I was going to get an A or, at lowest, maybe a B+ on the test.

ME DEMONSTRATING
MY AWESOME
BALLET TECHNIQUE

But, unfortunately, Chole and Zoey were too depressed to participate.

I was like, "Come on, guys, cheer up! We have to make up our ballet routine and practice it before we run out of time." But both of them just stared at me with big sad puppy-dog eyes.

"I can't believe our parents won't let us get tattoos! How unfair is that?" Chloe whined.

"And now Mrs. Peach will NEVER pick us for the trip to NYC! It's like our hopes and dreams have shriveled up and DIED!" Zoey sniffed, wiping a tear.

They spent the next forty-five minutes venting, and I, being the sensitive and caring friend that I am, sat quietly and listened.

Then the gym teacher came over and told us she was ready to start grading and we were going to be the second group to go. I just about had a heart attack because we hadn't selected any music or made up a routine.

I ran over really quick to grab a CD, and the only one left was *Swan Lake*. And since I had seen MacKenzie looking at it a few minutes earlier, I was definitely a little suspicious. So the first thing I did was pop open the CD case and peek inside. I was surprised and relieved to see that a CD was still in there. Hey, I didn't trust that girl as far as I could throw her.

MacKenzie's group was first, and I have to admit, they were pretty good. But it wasn't due to their awesome talent. Combined, the three of them had like eighty-nine years of private lessons. They danced to "Dance of the Sugar Plum Fairy" and ended their routine like this:

What a bunch of SHOW-OFFS! I mean, what real classically trained ballerina would end her dance by doing splits and cheesing (which, BTW, means smiling) like she just got her braces off or something. I was like, "Hey, girlfriends! This AIN'T *Dancing with the Stars!*" But I just said it inside my head, so one no else heard it but me.

We were up next, and I started getting butterflies in my stomach. Not because I was nervous. I just really hated humiliating myself in public. Chloe must have seen the look on my face because she whispered, "Don't panic! Just follow my lead. I took ballet lessons for three weeks back in second grade!" I said, "Thanks for sharing that, Chloe. Now I feel SO much better!" ☹

Then Zoey whispered, "What lies behind us and what lies before us are tiny matters compared to what lies within us. Ralph Waldo Emerson." Which, of course, had NOTHING WHATSOEVER to do with ANYTHING!

I had a really bad feeling about our routine, and

we hadn't even started it yet. Mainly because I discovered our *Swan Lake* CD was actually NOT a *Swan Lake* CD. It said *Swan Lake* on the case, but the CD inside said something else. When I read the title, I was like:

WHAT THE . . . ?!

It was *Thriller* by Michael Jackson!

Then my teacher snatched the CD out of my hand and popped it into her CD player and told us to take our places in front of the class.

I was about to explain that we had a slight complication with our music, but I got distracted when MacKenzie's group started squealing and hugging each other. They had gotten an A+ on their routine. But it was not like I was jealous or anything. I mean, how totally juvenile would *that* be?

Anyway, when our music came on, Chloe must have completely forgotten we were supposed to be doing a ballet routine because she started doing some funky dance moves like she was one of those half-rotted zombies from the *Thriller* music video.

The next thing I knew, Zoey was acting like a zombie too, so I didn't have a choice but to follow along. Plus, I figured our teacher would probably knock a few points off our grade if Chloe and Zoey were staggering around like the undead and I was doing ballet pliés in first and third position.

Okay. I really, really like Chloe and Zoey. But while I was up there dancing with them, I couldn't help thinking, "What am I? Flypaper for FREAKS?!"

I had to keep reminding myself that this whole thing was MacKenzie's fault, not THEIRS.

ME, CHLOE, AND ZOEY IN
BALLET OF THE ZOMBIES!

Actually, I was surprised that Chloe and Zoey were such good dancers. It looked like our gym teacher was pretty impressed too, because when we finished, she just stared at us with her mouth open and started tapping her ink pen on her clipboard really fast. Then she asked us to see her after class. We were really nervous when we went up to talk to her, because we didn't know what to expect. Chloe and Zoey thought maybe she was going to ask us to join the school's dance squad, since she was the assistant coach. I was keeping my fingers crossed on that one, because dance squad meant automatic membership in the CCP clique.

Our teacher smiled and said, "Girls, if we were doing the section on contemporary dance, you would have definitely gotten an A+!"

After hearing that, I was pretty sure she was going to give us a good grade on our routine even though we had made it up on the spot and with the wrong music.

Then our teacher stopped smiling.

"The three of you were supposed to be doing classical ballet, but you weren't even close. The highest grade I can give you is a D. I'm really sorry."

We were like, OH. NO. SHE. DIDN'T!!
Me, Chloe, and Zoey were CRUSHED! (LITERALLY.)

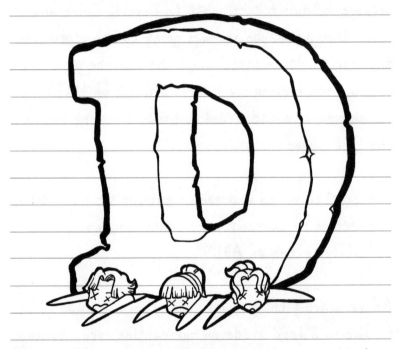

Then I screamed at my teacher, "Are you NUTS?! How in the world can you give us a D? Do you even realize how tricky those dance steps were? It was definitely A LOT harder than it looked! Let me see YOU try to moonwalk like a zombie, sister!"

But I just said all of that in my head, so no one heard it but me.

And get this! *Then* our teacher had the nerve to tell us to "hit the showers"! Like, what did showering have to do with classical ballet?! ABSOLUTELY NOTHING!!

I was a little peeved at Chloe and Zoey, because if they had NOT been wasting time whining about tattoos and National Library Week, we could have made up a decent ballet routine to the correct music and maybe earned at least a C. But NOOOOOO!

Then, at lunch, things went from bad to worse. Chloe and Zoey had a

TOTAL MELTDOWN!

They actually came up with this elaborate scheme to run away from home and live in the secret underground tunnels beneath the New York City Public Library!

But the crazy part was that they planned to leave this Friday, and then just "hang out" for seven whole months until National Library Week rolled around in April.

They figured that, by arriving early, they'd get in FREE and be FIRST in line for the author "Meet-n-Greet."

Chloe said residing at the library was going to be an "exhilarating experience," because they could read all the books they wanted, twenty-four hours a day, without having to check them out or reshelve them.

And Zoey said they were going to live off Diet Pepsi and nachos, which they planned to SWIPE from the library snack bar each night!

I CANNOT believe Chloe and Zoey are actually going to do something so crazy, dangerous, and illegal.

CHLOE AND ZOEY USING THEIR NATURAL INSTINCTS TO SCAVENGE FOR FOOD

And I plan to do everything within my power to STOP them!

WHY?!

Because Chloe and Zoey are my BEST friends at this school!

And my ONLY friends at this school! But that's beside the point.

Unfortunately, I only have TWO options:

1. Rat them out to their 'rents and risk losing their friendship forever

OR

2. Figure out a way to get girlfriends some tattoos for National Library Week PDQ (which, BTW, means "pretty darn quick")!!

I hardly got any sleep last night! I kept having horrible nightmares about Chloe and Zoey living in the secret underground tunnels beneath the NYC public library.

In one of my dreams, they were having a dinner party with some of their neighbors.

And in the scariest one, I got married to Brandon Roberts and Chloe and Zoey were bridesmaids. But they brought a few uninvited guests to my wedding ☹!

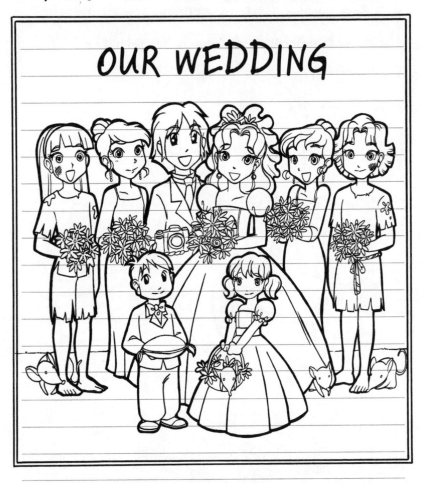

OUR WEDDING

I actually woke up SCREAMING my head off until I realized it was all just a very bad dream!

This morning at breakfast my little sister, Brianna, got on my last nerve.

I was just sitting there, eating my Cinnamon Life, reading the back of the cereal box, and trying to figure out what I was going to do about the Chloe and Zoey situation.

They were planning to leave in less than twenty-four hours.

Brianna was eating Fruity Pebbles and drawing a face on her hand with an ink pen. She said she was naming the face "Miss Penelope" because she was "borned from a pen."

BRIANNA'S HAND

Even though I was trying to concentrate on my personal problems, Miss Penelope asked me to watch her perform "Itsy-Bitsy Spider," the Rihanna remix version.

Apparently, the itsy-bitsy spider went up the water spout but got washed out by the rain because he had no umbrella, ella ella, eh, eh, eh!

The whole thing annoyed me to no end, because I wasn't that into puppet shows.

Anyway, I warned both Brianna and Miss Penelope to quit bothering me, mainly because I was in a really

HORRIBLE MOOD.

And it was not helping matters that Miss Penelope's awful singing sounded like a humpback whale in labor.

She must have been highly insulted by my unbiased critique of her singing abilities, because she hauled off and socked me on my arm.

So I grabbed Miss Penelope and tried to drown her in my cereal bowl.

I was like,

"Got milk?!"

Brianna started screaming, "Stop it! Miss Penelope can't swim! Let her go! You're smushing her face!"

But I wouldn't let go. That is, until my mom walked into the kitchen.

"Why on Earth are you shoving your sister's hand in your cereal?! LET GO OF HER THIS INSTANT!!"

So I released Miss Penelope only because I didn't have a choice.

Brianna stuck her tongue out at me. "Miss Penelope says she's not inviting you to her birthday party! Na, na, na, na, na!!"

Then I stuck my tongue out at *her* and said, "I've *already* not been invited to a birthday party. SO THERE!" I could thank MacKenzie for that one.

Anyway, I think I taught Miss Penelope a good lesson. I bet she won't be interrupting my breakfast again anytime soon (EVIL GRIN).

Since my cereal had been contaminated by Miss Penelope's germs, I dumped it into the sink and ran upstairs to my bedroom.

I sat on my bed and stared at my wall as a million thoughts bounced around in my head.

I had to admit, the Chloe and Zoey situation seemed hopeless, and there was nothing I could do to fix it ☹.

To make matters worse, Miss Penelope was still in

the kitchen singing so off-key, I thought my ears were going to bleed. I felt like taking my favorite pen—a water-based, nontoxic, dark purple gel ink pen by HotWriter, Inc.—and drawing a big fat zipper across her mouth to shut her up. But I was pretty sure my mom would have just YELLED at me again.

I mainly just use it to write in my diary and to bring me good luck. But lately, the good luck part hasn't been working so well.

MY LUCKY PEN

I was twirling my pen in my fingers when, suddenly, the CRAZIEST idea popped into my head! I was like, OMG! This might work! I quickly scribbled out two notes and then rushed off to school fifteen minutes early to tape them on Chloe's and Zoey's lockers.

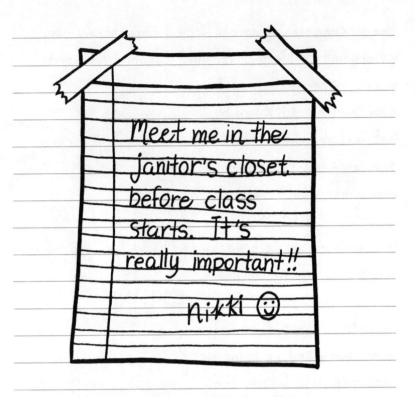

Meet me in the
janitor's closet
before class
Starts. It's
really important!!

nikki ☺

I waited in the janitor's closet for five long minutes
and was starting to worry they were not going to
show up. But finally they did.

"I hope you didn't ask us to come here to try and
change our minds about running away," Chloe said,
real seriouslike.

"Yeah! This is something we just gotta do," Zoey
said, staring at the floor.

It got so sad and quiet, I thought I was going
to cry.

"Um . . . I asked you both to come here to
tell you about a special present I wanted to give
you on Monday. But since you're leaving
tomorrow . . ."

Of course, this made Chloe and Zoey really curious,
and they started begging me to tell them what
it was.

"Well, you may not know this, but I'm a pretty
decent artist. Not that I'm bragging or anything.
And since you guys are my BFFs, I've decided to
personally give you each a tattoo! Temporary ones. In
honor of National Library Week!"

At first Chloe and Zoey just stared at me like
they couldn't believe it.

Then they started screaming and jumping up and
down and hugging me.

ME, CHLOE, AND ZOEY DOING A GROUP HUG!

"Just decide what kind you want," I said, "and I'll design it over the weekend and draw it during lunch on Monday. But you both have to make me one promise . . ."

"Anything!!" Zoey gushed. "Let me guess! We have to ditch our plans to run away and live at the NYC library?"

"Okay, then it's officially CANCELED!" Chloe announced, and did jazz hands, like the show was over.

"Actually, that's not what I meant," I said, hiding my smile and trying to look all scary-serious. "I want you both to promise me you won't bring RATS to my wedding!"

"HUH?!" They both looked at me like I was crazy.

"Never mind!" I giggled. "It's a long story."

Before biology class started, I noticed Brandon was kind of staring at me, but I wasn't sure if it was my imagination or not. Lately, it seemed like whenever I looked at *HIM*, he was looking at *ME*.

But then we both would look away and pretend like we WEREN'T really looking at each other.

Well, today he actually smiled at me and said, "So, which cell cycle would you rather study? Mitosis or meiosis?"

I smiled back and kind of shrugged my shoulders because actually, I HATED both of them EQUALLY. And I was afraid that anything I said would probably make me look like a BIGGER idiot than he already thought I was.

But the main reason I couldn't talk to Brandon was because I was suffering from a very severe and debilitating case of RCS, or Roller-Coaster Syndrome. Studies show that it mainly attacks girls between the ages of eight and sixteen.

The symptoms are difficult to describe, but whenever Brandon talks to me, my stomach feels like I'm dropping nine hundred feet at eighty miles per hour. Simply calling it "butterflies" is a common and dangerous misdiagnosis.

Suddenly, and without warning, I feel compelled to throw my hands up in the air (like I just don't care) and scream . . .

"WHEEEEEE!"

ME RIDING THE
LOVE ROLLER
COASTER!!
I so
LOVE to HATE
this feeling
☺!!

Then my day got even BETTER! While I was working in the library, Brandon came in to return a book called *Photography and You*. I was just sitting there, doodling a few tattoo designs for Chloe and Zoey, when he leaned across the counter and peeked at my notebook.

"Now *that* is good! I didn't know you were an artist!"

I looked around to see who he was talking to. Then, I totally freaked out when I realized he was actually talking to ME! I could hardly BREATHE.

"Thanks, but it's no big deal. I've been going to art camp like forever. And last summer, I got practically a million mosquito bites and wow, did they ever itch!!" I babbled like an idiot.

"Well, one thing is for sure, you definitely got skillz!"

Brandon's hair was hanging in his eyes again as he smiled and kind of leaned in even closer to look

178

at my sketches. I thought I was going to DIE! He smelled like Snuggle fabric softener, Axe body spray, and . . . red licorice?!

I couldn't stop blushing, and there was no way I could draw with him watching me like that. I started feeling that roller-coaster thing all over again . . . WHEEEEE!

Suddenly Brandon's eyes seemed to twinkle with excitement.

"Hey! Are you entering the avant-garde art competition? I'll be covering it for the newspaper."

"Yeah, I'm thinking about it. But everyone is saying MacKenzie's fashion illustrations are going to win this year. So I dunno . . ."

"MacKenzie?! Are you kidding? You have more talent in your smallest burp than she has in her entire body. I'm serious! You know that, right?"

I could NOT believe Brandon actually said that! It

was so rude. So wickedly funny. So . . . TRUE!

We both laughed really hard. I didn't know he had such a wacky sense of humor.

Soon, Chloe and Zoey came staggering up to the front desk, each loaded down with a stack of books that needed to be put away.

When they saw us, their mouths dropped open.

They looked at me, then at Brandon, then at me again. Then at Brandon. Then back at me. Then Brandon. Then me. Then Brandon again.

This went on like FOREVER!

They were gawking at us like we were a new animal exhibit at the zoo or something.

It was SO embarrassing!

Brandon's smile went slightly crooked, but otherwise, he acted coolly nonchalant about the whole thing.

"HEY, GET A LOAD OF THOSE TWO!
IT MUST BE MATING SEASON OR SOMETHING . . ."

"Hey, Chloe! Hey, Zoey!" he said.

But they were so shocked, they didn't even answer him.

"Well, I better get back to class. See you later, Nikki." Then he strolled out the door and disappeared into the hall.

Chloe and Zoey made a big deal over Brandon talking to me like that and started nagging me to admit he was my secret crush.

After I made them both pinkie swear not to tell anyone, I told them about how Brandon had helped me up after Jessica tripped me in the cafeteria a couple of weeks ago.

Then I grabbed my backpack and unzipped the cute little pocket in the front and showed them The Napkin.

At first they just stared at it in awe. But soon they were teasing me and giggling like two kindergarteners. "Brandon and Nikki sittin' in a tree, K-I-S-S-I-N-G!"

I told them to shut up before someone overheard them and it got out all over the school.

Chloe insisted that I keep The Napkin for the rest of my life, because there was a chance that Brandon and I could accidentally meet up on some exotic, romantic island twenty years from now. She said it could happen just like it did in those chick flicks at the movie theater.

MY BEST FRIEND'S NAPKIN
(SLEEPLESS IN SAN DIEGO)
Directed by Chloe Christina Garcia

BRANDON:
I couldn't help but notice you from across the room and be hopelessly drawn to your brains and beauty! It almost seems that we've met before. Perhaps in another place . . . another time . . . another life . . . !

ME:
Alas! Allergy season is upon us. Please! Take this most cherished napkin from my very heart-wrenching, mysterious past.
And do with it . . . what you must!!

ME:
What a powerful sneeze you have!
It is aptly captured in this delicate
napkin of forgotten love . . . now
merely a disposable tissue drenched
in lost and shattered dreams!

BRANDON:
Hark! Do mine eyes deceive
me?! I'd recognize OUR
napkin in even the darkest
of murky depths! My joy
and passion overwhelm me!

BRANDON:
Is it really you? My beloved,
Nikki! Finally, I've found
my TRUE LOVE! Will you
MARRY ME?!

THE END

I told Chloe her story was really sweet and romantic. But if the napkin was really dripping with snot and Brandon proposed on the spot like that, MY story would probably have a different ending.

ME:
Gee, Brandon, I think we need to take things a bit slower. First, let's get rid of the snotty napkin . . . ICK!! Second, how about pizza and a movie . . . ?

THE END

Zoey said she didn't blame me for rewriting Chloe's happy ending, because snot and airborne bacterial particles were the most common way of transmitting germs to others.

But Chloe complained we both *TOTALLY* missed her point. The Napkin, germy or not, should be cherished because it was a token of Brandon's love. And after reading *Twilight*, she had learned that forbidden love, obsession, and sacrifice could be very messy things. Just like snot.

I had to admit that Chloe had a really good point.

Then Zoey said I should always remember that guys are from Mars and girls are from Venus, because they think and communicate very differently, according to a book she was reading on dating. I was really surprised to hear this, because I thought for sure that Earth was the only planet with human life on it.

I'm really glad Chloe and Zoey know so much

about guys, dating, love, and stuff like that.

Because I don't have a CLUE.

DUH!!

SATURDAY, SEPTEMBER 28

This is going to be my LONGEST diary entry EVER! I have the most horrible headache, and it's all Brianna's fault. Why, why, why couldn't I have been born an ONLY child?!

Okay. This is what happened: My mom and Brianna were supposed to see a matinee movie today. But Mom needed to go to the mall to buy a present for a baby shower she was attending later this evening.

So she offered me $10 to take Brianna to the movie in her place. Since I was broke, I agreed to do it. I figured that, at the worst, I could sleep through the movie and earn $10 for a ninety-minute nap.

The movie was called *Princess Sugar Plum Saves Baby Unicorn Island! Part 3.* There must have been four hundred squealing little girls there, and half of them were dressed up like princesses and unicorns.

I should have charged my mom $50 for taking Brianna, because the whole event was so sugary sweet, it actually made me nauseous.

But Brianna thought the movie was superscary because there was a fairy in it. And she has this irrational fear that the tooth fairy is going to pull out all her teeth to make dentures for old people. I guess you could say she suffers from "fairy phobia."

Anyway, Brianna practically drove me CRAZY, because every time the fairy appeared on the screen, she got really scared, grabbed my arm, and bumped my popcorn.

I must have dumped three whole boxes on the nice lady sitting next to me.

But when that nice lady looked like she was going to slug me, I decided it would be safer to eat Raisinets instead.

I was TOO happy when that stupid movie was finally over.

Brianna and I were waiting near the main entrance for Mom to pick us up. However, when I saw Dad pull up in his Maxwell's Bug Extermination van, I got a really bad feeling. Although, that creepy-looking roach bolted to the top of his van gave *most* people a really bad feeling.

BTW, the roach's name is Max (courtesy of Brianna, "because if I had a puppy, I'd name him Max").

I was like, OH CRUD! If anyone from my school saw me getting into Dad's van, my life would be over. I scanned the crowd for middle school kids, and

luckily, it was still mostly three- to six-year-olds.
"Hi, girls, hop in! Your mom's still shopping. I just got
an emergency call, so you get to ride along to keep
me company," my dad said, winking.

I was like, "Um . . . thanks, Dad, but I have an awful
lot of homework to do. So could you just drop me
home first! PLEASE!" I was trying really hard to
remain calm.

My dad glanced at his watch and frowned. "Sorry,
but I don't have time to swing by the house. This
customer is hysterical and has agreed to pay my
emergency rates. She's hosting some kind of big
shindig later today and says her house is crawling
with bugs inside and out. Hundreds of 'em just
showed up out of the blue this morning."

"ICK!!" Brianna said, scrunching up her nose.

"Sounds like a box elder infestation to me." Dad
continued, "Hopefully, she's not throwing that baby
shower your mom is supposed to be attending later
today."

I grumpily climbed into the front seat of the van and tried to slouch down really low so no one could see me.

Whenever we stopped at a red light, a bunch of people would point, stare, and laugh. Not at me; at our roach.

For some reason, Brianna thought all the gawkers were just being friendly. So she started smiling, waving, and throwing kisses out the window like she had just been crowned Miss America or something.

And Dad was pretty used to all the rude stares. He just ignored them and hummed along to his *Saturday Night Fever* CD.

Thank goodness I noticed an empty grocery bag sticking out from under the seat.

Even though it said WARNING: TO AVOID SERIOUS INJURY OR DEATH, PLEASE KEEP PLASTIC AWAY FROM VERY YOUNG CHILDREN! I poked two eye holes in it and pulled it down over my head.

First of all, I *WASN'T* a very young child.

And second of all, I'd rather suffer a slow and painful death by asphyxiation than be spotted riding around in the "roachmobile"!

I have to admit, we probably looked like a

FREAK SHOW ON WHEELS.

It was SO embarrassing!

I wondered how serious my injuries would be if I jumped from a moving vehicle traveling forty-five

193

miles per hour. Assuming I survived, I could at least walk home and end the humiliating ride in Dad's van.

About ten minutes later, we drove up a long driveway that led to a huge house. Wow! Nice house, I thought. Too bad it has bugs!

Brianna stared at the house in awe. "Daddy, can I go inside with you? Pretty please!"

"Sorry, pumpkin, but you'll have to wait out here in the van with your sister and make sure no one steals Max, okay?"

Like WHO in their right mind would want MAX?!

Two shiny black bugs about a half inch long landed on the window of our van.

"Yep! Box elders all right," Dad said, eyeing them carefully. "Basically just a harmless eyesore. To spray the entire premises will probably take about twenty minutes. But I'll try to get it done as fast as I can. If you girls need anything, I'll be right inside."

Dad unloaded his equipment and lugged it up the front steps. Before he could ring the doorbell, a frantic-looking middle-aged lady in designer clothing opened the door and ushered him in.

Brianna started to pout. "I wanna go in there with DAD!"

"NO! You're supposed to stay here. And watch Max! Remember?" I said sternly.

Brianna wrinkled her nose at me.

"YOU watch Max! I gotta go to the bathroom!"

"Brianna, Dad will be back real soon. Can't you just hold it a little longer?"

"NO! I gotta go NOOOWW!"

I was like, Just great! All of this drama for a measly $10.

"Okay, fine," I said, finally giving in. "When we go

inside, don't touch anything. Just use the bathroom and come right out, got that?"

"I wanna say hi to Dad too!"

"No! You're gonna use the bathroom, and then we're coming back to the van to wait for . . ."

Before I could finish my sentence, Brianna slid open the van door and dashed to the front steps.

By the time I caught up with her, she was already leaning on the doorbell. "Ding-dong! Ding-dong! Ding-dong!"

The flustered-looking lady answered the door again and looked surprised to see Brianna and me.

"Um . . . I really apologize for disturbing you," I stammered. "But we were out in the van waiting for our dad and—"

"Hey, lady! I gotta go PEEEEEEE!" Brianna interrupted.

Then she started squirming and making ugly faces for maximum dramatic effect.

The lady looked at Brianna, then at me, and then back at Brianna. She stretched her thin red lips into a strained smile.

"Oh! So your dad is our . . . exterminator. Sure,

honey, the bathroom is right this way. Follow me."

The inside of the house looked like something out of one of my mom's fancy home and garden magazines. We were headed down a hallway off the foyer when the lady stopped in her tracks.

"Oh, wait! There's bug spray in all the bathrooms on the main floor. You're going to have to use one upstairs. All of the bedrooms have an attached bathroom. I'd escort you myself, but my caterer is supposed to call me any minute now for a final head count."

The telephone rang, and the lady gasped and rushed off, leaving us standing there. Brianna smiled and darted up the huge staircase ahead of me.

As she entered the first bedroom on the right, she squealed with glee, "Ooh! Pretty!"

It was decorated in shades of pink and had plush carpeting soft enough to sleep on. The laptop and big-screen TV were to die for. My entire bedroom could fit into the walk-in closet. But, personally, it was a little too sugar-n-spice for my taste. Not that I was jealous or anything. Like how juvenile would THAT be?!

ME AND BRIANNA IN TOTAL AWE OF THE FABULOUS BEDROOM!! (WHICH, BTW, TOOK ME LIKE FOREVER TO DRAW!!)

"Hey! Can I jump up and down on this princessy bed?!" Brianna asked.

"NO!" I snapped. "Get down!"

It took all my willpower not to snoop. I wondered what school the girl attended and if we could ever be friends. I bet she had a perfect life. Unlike me.

Brianna skipped into the adjoining bathroom and locked the door behind her. "Wow, I'm gonna get a bathroom like this for my birthday!"

Soon, I heard the toilet flush. But after three minutes, she still had not come out.

"Brianna, hurry up!!" I shouted through the door.

"Wait, I'm still washing my hands really good with this strawberry soap, and then I'm going to put on some yummy-smelling cupcake body spray."

"Come on. We have to go back to the van now."

"Wait!! I'm almost done!"

Suddenly I heard a sickeningly familiar voice.

"But, Mommm! I CAN'T have my party with these horrible BUGS crawling all over! We should have had it at the country club like I wanted. This is totally YOUR fault!"

I almost wet my pants! It was MACKENZIE ☹!

I was like, OMG! OMG! OMG! Today was the party I had not been invited to.

It was like a demented nightmare. I was trapped in MacKenzie's bedroom, my sister was locked in MacKenzie's bathroom, and my dad was exterminating MacKenzie's house. And if *all* that wasn't awful enough, our van, with a humongous roach on top of it, was parked in MacKenzie's driveway with MY last name plastered across the side of it (the van, not the roach).

I wanted to dig a deep hole in the lush pink carpet, crawl into it, and DIE! I pounded on the door.

BAM!
BAM!

ME
(HAVING A
MELTDOWN!)

"BRIANNA! COME ON! OPEN UP!"

"I'm busy. Go away!"

"You've been in there long enough. Now open the door!"

"Say 'pretty please.'"

"Pretty please."

"Now say 'pretty please with sugar on top.'"

"Okay. Open the door, pretty please with sugar on top . . ."

"NO!! I'm NOT done yet!"

"Mommm! This party is going to be a DISASTER! My reputation will be ruined! We *have* to cancel it."

I could hear MacKenzie's shrieks getting louder. She was coming up the stairs!

"Brianna. Open the door quick! PLEASE! It's an emergency!" I hissed through the door.

"Wait! I'm putting on the yummy-smelling cupcake body spray now. Um . . . what's the emergency?"

Now MacKenzie was in the hallway.

"Mom, I'm calling Jessica. She'll never believe this is happening to me . . ."

I had exactly three seconds to convince Brianna to open the bathroom door.

"Brianna! It's the TOOTH FAIRY! She's coming, and we have to get out of here!! NOW!!"

The lock on the door clicked, and Brianna whipped open the door.

She looked even more afraid than she had been at the *Princess Sugar Plum* movie.

"D-did you say T-T-TOOTH FAIRY?!"

"Yes! Come on, let's HIDE! Quick!"

Brianna was panicking and starting to whine.

"Where is she? I'm scared! I want Daaaaaddy!"

"Let's hide behind the shower curtain. If we're really quiet, she'll never find us."

Brianna shut up instantly, but her eyes were as big as saucers.

I actually felt a little sorry for her.

We dove into the bathtub and huddled behind the shower curtain.

I could hear MacKenzie stomping around her bedroom and screaming into her cell phone.

"Jess, there's no way I can have this party now! Our house is crawling with bugs! What? . . . How am I supposed to know what they are? They're these big black, er . . . roaches or something. Some guy is here spraying, but now the house stinks! It STINKS, Jess! How can I have a party with the house STINKING!"

"Nikki, I'm a-scared. I want my daaad-dy! NOW!"

"I BEGGED Mom to let me have my party at the country club! Lyndsey's mom let her have her party at the country club. But NOOO! Getting my mom to do anything these days is like pulling TEETH!"

WHY did MacKenzie have to say the T word?!

Brianna totally lost it and started climbing out of the tub.

"OH NO! Did you hear that! She's says she's going to pull out my TEETH! I wanna go hooome!"

"Brianna!! Wait . . . !" I tackled her and held her in a headlock. Finally, she stopped squirming and went limp.

Then the little brat BIT me!! HARD! I let go of her and yelped in pain like a wounded animal. "YEEOOOOW!" But I did it inside my head, so no one else heard it but me.

Brianna scrambled out of the tub, opened the bathroom door, and disappeared into MacKenzie's bedroom!

I froze and held my breath. I could not believe this was happening to me.

Then I thought, maybe this is just a nightmare. Like those scary-weird dreams I was having earlier in the week about Chloe and Zoey. If I could just wake up, this would ALL go away.

So I closed my eyes, pinched myself really hard, and tried to wake up.

But when I opened my eyes, I was *still* standing in

MacKenzie's bathtub, with Brianna's (now black-and-blue) teeth marks on my arm, next to a throbbing red pinch mark.

I SO wished I was DEAD!

Suddenly, another idea popped into my head. If I turned on MacKenzie's shower and stood under freezing cold water for an hour, I might die of pneumonia. But even that could take a few days, and I needed to be DEAD, RIGHT NOW!

"OMG! Jess, there's a little KID in my room! . . . How would I know? She appeared out of nowhere. I've told Amanda a million times my room is off-limits to her and her pesky little friends. Hold on . . ."

"MOM . . . !! Amanda and her friends are playing in my room again! Would you please do something . . . ?!"

"Okay, Jess, I'm back. If they so much as touch my makeup again, I swear, I'm going to strangle . . ."

"Don't you dare touch me you, you . . . WICKED

tooth fairy!" Brianna screamed at the top of her lungs.

Suddenly I felt really light-headed. I was sure I was about to faint.

"Hold on a minute, Jess . . ."

"WHO told you I was the tooth fairy? WHAT are you doing in my bedroom? And WHERE is Amanda?!!"

"You can't have my tooths! NEVER!" Brianna shouted bravely.

"MOM!! AMANDA!! Hold on, Jess. I have to get rid of this little kid. Then I'm going to KILL Amanda! Okay. Outta my room, right this—"

"STOP! Let go of me! I LOVE my tooths!"

There was a loud thump, and MacKenzie shrieked.

"MOM! I've just been attacked by a demonic munchkin! OMG! I think I'm bruised! I can't wear my new

OOOW! YOU LITTLE...!

← BRIANNA BATTLING THE WICKED TOOTH FAIRY!

Jimmy Choo flip-flops with a big bruise on my leg!"

"Are you still there, Jess? I can't have my party like this. I've got a bruise the size of a pancake. NO! . . . I didn't get bruised by a pancake! I said . . . Hold on . . . !"

I could hear MacKenzie hobbling down the stairs like a one-legged pirate. Click-klunk, click-klunk, click-klunk.

"MOM! Last week Amanda and her friends put gum in my hair and colored with my lipsticks! Now one of them just . . ."

When it sounded like MacKenzie's screeches were coming from a safe distance away, I jumped out of the bathtub, grabbed Brianna, and tossed her over my shoulder like a sack of rotten potatoes.

Without stopping even once, I hauled her down the stairs, through the hall, to the foyer, and out the front door.

I deposited her butt in the backseat of the van and slammed the door.

My dad was in the back, loading up his equipment.

"Oh, there you girls are! Perfect timing. I'm all done."

As Dad started the van and drove off, I stared at the house, half expecting MacKenzie to come limping out the front door ranting that Brianna be arrested for creating a bruise that prevented her from wearing her new Jimmy Choos at her birthday party. Amazingly, Brianna sat calmly in the backseat and seemed quite pleased with herself.

"Daddy, guess what? I went to use the bathroom, and after I washed my hands with strawberry soap and put on cupcake body spray, I saw the tooth fairy with rollers in her hair talking on a fairy phone, and she said she was going to strangle me and pull out all of my teeth to make dentures for old people. So when she grabbed me, I kicked her and she let go and started screaming for her mommy. Then she flew back to fairyland to go to a party for Jimmy Shoe. She's not so nice, that's for sure! I like Santa and the Easter Bunny much better."

Lucky for us, Dad was only half listening to Brianna's rambling. "Really, pumpkin? So is that what your *Princess Sugar Plum* movie was about?"

At the next stoplight, I noticed a carload of teen

boys pointing and laughing. I put my plastic bag back over my head and slouched down in the seat.

I was so mad I could SPIT!

All of this drama for a measly ten bucks!!

I'm starting to get really excited because the avant-garde art competition is only eight days away! I decided to enter my watercolor painting that took me two whole summers at art camp to complete. I spent more than 130 hours on it.

The only complication is that I gave it to my mom and dad last spring for their sixteenth wedding anniversary. So it's technically not mine anymore. It was either my painting or spending my entire life savings of $109.21 to buy them dinner at a fancy restaurant.

But I knew the dinner was going to be a total rip-off, because I watch the Food Network. All of those five-star restaurants serve really gross stuff like frog legs and snails, and then give you a tiny portion on a really big plate with chocolate syrup drizzled over it and a garnish. And "garnish" is just a fancy name for a plain old piece of parsley.

So, to save money, Brianna and I decided to cook

a romantic candlelit dinner for Mom and Dad as an anniversary surprise. We took a big bucket and a net to the pond at the park and hunted down some fresh frog legs and snails.

It was MY brilliant idea to make it an all-you-can-eat buffet, since we were basically getting the food for FREE.

CHEF NIKKI AND HER ASSISTANT PREPARE A TASTY GOURMET DINNER OF FROG LEGS AND SNAILS

ME PLAYING WITH MY FOOD ↓

LOVE AT FIRST SIGHT ↓

SAUCE →

Chocolate Syrup

RUNAWAY SNAIL ↑

PARSLEY ↑

FRESH FROG LEGS ↑

FRESH SNAILS ↑

Trying to prepare a gourmet dinner was definitely a lot harder than I thought it would be. The frogs kept jumping out of the bowl, and the snails wouldn't stay on the plate. Unfortunately, none of those shows on the Food Network explained how to control all the critters while you're trying to cook 'em.

And Brianna was no help WHATSOEVER! She was *supposed* to be my assistant, but she kept swiping the frogs and kissing them to see if they'd turn into princes. I scolded her really good about that because she had NO IDEA where those frogs' lips had been!

Not surprisingly, Brianna threw a big hissy fit when it came time to put the food in the oven. She said they were her friends and "friends DON'T COOK friends!" I had to admit, she DID have a good point. So we decided to take Mom and Dad's anniversary dinner back to the pond and let them go. I guess you could say they were really lucky. "They" meaning the frogs and snails, not Mom and Dad.

Since our dinner plans fell through, and I didn't

want to part with my life savings, I stuck a big red Christmas bow on my watercolor painting and used that as a gift instead. Mom and Dad must have really loved it, because they paid a ton of money to have it professionally matted and put into an expensive antique frame. Then they hung it in our living room, right over the couch.

Even though it's now a priceless family heirloom with tremendous sentimental value, Mom said I could borrow it for the avant-garde art competition as long as I took really good care of it.

I was like, "Mom, don't worry! Nothing's going to happen. I'll be supercareful. I PROMISE!"

It's JUST an art show. I mean, WHAT could go wrong?!

I couldn't believe that MacKenzie actually came to school on crutches today. She even stuck little heart stickers on them so that they matched her new Gucci hobo handbag. Only someone as vain as MacKenzie would try to look CUTE while hobbling around on crutches. She didn't have a cast on her leg or anything. Just a SpongeBob Band-Aid below her left knee. HOW FAKE IS THAT?!!

According to the latest gossip, MacKenzie was taking scuba diving lessons on Saturday from this really hot ninth grader when she "ruptured her shin" while saving him from drowning. She supposedly did mouth-to-mouth resuscitation on him until the ambulance arrived. And since the poor guy's dying wish was for her to escort him to the hospital, she was forced to cancel her birthday party. So she rescheduled it for Saturday, October 12th at her parents' country club. I was like, Yeah, RIGHT!

MacKenzie is such a LIAR and a DRAMA QUEEN! Why couldn't she just tell the truth and admit her party was canceled because her house was infested with bugs and stank from bug spray?

Anyway, today I could hardly wait for lunch. Chloe and Zoey were even more excited than I was. We sat at our usual table and snarfed down our lunch as fast as we could.

Then I rolled up Zoey's sleeve, took out my lucky pen, and got started on her tattoo. She kept giggling and squirming and saying it tickled. I said,

"LISTEN, ZOEY, SHUT UP AND SIT STILL OR I'M GONNA TURN ANY STRAY INK MARKS INTO UGLY BABY SNAKES!!"

Lucky for her, she stopped moving after that.

Practically everyone in the cafeteria was staring at us, but I ignored them and kept right on working. Zoey's tattoo turned out really cool, and she loved it.

I was just getting started on Chloe's tattoo when the weirdest thing happened.

Jason Feldman got up, left the CCP table, and sat down at OUR table to watch. He's just *THE* most popular guy in the entire school and president of the student council.

On the cuteness scale, I would say he was a 9.93 out of 10.

"You're doing a tattoo with a pen?! Cool! It looks so real. I should know because my brother just got one for his eighteenth birthday."

"It's our special LSA project for National Library Week," Chloe said, and batted her eyelashes at him all flirtylike.

"Yeah! And all the latest fashion magazines say tattoos are HAWT!" Zoey added in this really nasally voice that sounded a lot like Paris Hilton.

Those two were acting so phony-baloney, it was sickening. I thought I was going to puke up my lunch right in Jason's lap.

"So what do I have to do to get one?" Jason asked excitedly. "Donate a book or something? Do you have a sign-up sheet?"

Zoey's and Chloe's faces lit up at the same time,

and I could see the little lightbulb click on in their brains.

I just sighed and rolled my eyes. First it was the tattoo thing, then *Ballet of the Zombies,* and then running away to live in the secret underground tunnels at the NYC public library.

I didn't know if I could put up with much more of this drama.

Chloe fluttered her eyelashes at Jason again. "Well, Nikki is art director, I'm overseeing book procurement, and Zoey here handles scheduling. Zoey, would you please give Jason our sign-up sheet?"

"Er . . . what sign-up sheet?" Zoey asked, looking confused.

Chloe winked at her and said really loudly, "You know, the *SIGN-UP SHEET* in your *NOTEBOOK,* silly!"

Finally, Zoey caught on. "Oh, *THAT* sign-up sheet! Of course!" She gazed at Jason and giggled nervously.

Zoey whipped out her notebook, tore out a sheet of paper, scribbled TATTOO SIGN-UP SHEET across the top, and handed it to Chloe.

Chloe added the words BOOK DONATION REQUIRED (NEW OR USED)!! in big bold letters and gave it to Jason.

I was shocked and appalled to see Chloe and Zoey lying like that. I always felt honesty was a very important quality in a friend.

Jason scrawled his name on the sign-up sheet and then yelled to his lunch table on the other side of the cafeteria, "Hey, Crenshaw! Get Thompson and come check this out."

Ryan Crenshaw was a 9.86, and Matt Thompson was a 9.98. They both came over and sat down at OUR table, right next to Jason.

Then the three of them started laughing and talking to me, Chloe, and Zoey like we were CCP girls or something.

That's when I decided that, although an honest friend was nice, an "I-can-hook-you-up-with-really-cute-guys" friend was far better.

And besides, Chloe and Zoey weren't actually lying. They were just over-embellishing some fabricated truths.

Even though I was enjoying all of the unexpected attention, there was an incessant gnawing deep down inside my gut that had me really worried.

WHY were the three most popular CCP guys suddenly sitting at a lunch table, flirting with Chloe, Zoey, and me, the three biggest DORKS in the school?

And WHAT exactly did they want from us?

Then I had to force myself to ponder the most

INTRIGUING and TROUBLING question of all . . .

Was my lucky pen going
to MELT from all of
the CCP GUY
HOTNESS?!

Here are the THREE reasons why I was a little
worried about my pen . . .

JASON (The Prep)   RYAN (The Jock)   MATT (The Bad Boy)

Within minutes, seven more guys had crashed our
table and were passing around the sign-up sheet
and boasting about how wicked their tat was going
to be.

I finally finished up Chloe's tattoo, and she said it was perfect.

Reading is Magical

Jason rolled up his sleeve and took Chloe's place.

"Hey, dudes. Listen up! Mine is gonna say, 'GUITAR HERO'!!"

All of the guys started slapping him on the back and giving him high fives and fist bumps. He was acting all smug, like he was getting a new sports car or something.

Then a large crowd of girls gathered around the large crowd of guys to watch me work on Jason's tattoo.

"Isn't she the new girl?"

"I think her locker is right next to MacKenzie's."

"She's like _THE_ best artist in the entire school."

"Hey, I wanna sign up! Give me the sheet next . . ."

"What's her name?"

"Mikki, Rikki, or Vicki, I think."

"Whatever her name is, the girl's got SKILLZ."

"I'm SOOO jealous! I can't draw a stick figure."

"She's in my French class. Her name is Nikki Maxwell!"

"I'd LOVE to draw on Jason Feldman. He's HAWT!"

"OMG! I'd give ANYTHING to be Nikki Maxwell!"

I was starting to feel like a POP STAR!

The only CCPs not at our table were MacKenzie
and her little group. They were GLARING at us
from across the cafeteria.

By the end of lunch period, I had completed seven
tattoos, Chloe had collected nine books, and Zoey
had scheduled eleven people to get tattoos tomorrow
at lunch.

We decided to call our new LSA project:

"Ink Exchange: Trade a Book for a Tattoo!"

In no time, the ENTIRE school was gossiping about it.

Mrs. Peach said collecting books for charity was a wonderful idea, and she was really proud of us. Brandon even congratulated me and said he wanted to interview me for the school newspaper on Friday since I was "breaking news." He said he planned to photograph a few students showing off their new tattoos for the article. Now I can hardly wait for Friday to get here ☺! There's a chance we might actually become good friends.

But the absolute, most mind-blowing thing about all of this is that Chloe, Zoey, and I started the school day as LSA DORKS and ended it as CCP DIVAS!

HOW COOL IS THAT?! ☺!!

TUESDAY, OCTOBER 1

	Today	Total
TATTOOS	17	24
BOOKS	34	43

This tattoo craze has really caught on at WCD!
I did eleven more during lunch, and most of the
CCPs sat at our table to watch. It was pretty cool
hanging out with them, and they were not mean or
snotty like we thought they'd be. I guess it was just
a matter of getting to know them better.

Surprisingly, I ended up doing another six tattoos
while I was on LSA duty. It seemed like everyone
and their mother was getting library passes during
fifth-hour homeroom and pestering me.

But Mrs. Peach said she didn't mind me not shelving
books, since I was working on our group project.

So far, we've collected a total of forty-three books
for charity, which is fantastic. But it was mainly
because Chloe decided to start charging two books

per tattoo instead of one. Zoey and I thought one book was perfectly fine, and we told her so.

But Chloe said that, since she was the director of book procurement, it was her decision, not ours, so it didn't matter what we thought. Now, how RUDE was THAT?!

I was like, "Okay, Chloe! We're supposed to be doing this as a group project! Who DIED and made you QUEEN?!"

CHLOE THE GREAT, QUEEN OF BOOKS →

But I just said it in my head, so no one else heard it but me. So now we're getting TWO books for each tattoo, although it seems a bit GREEDY, if you ask me. ☹!

WEDNESDAY, OCTOBER 2

	Today	Total
TATTOOS	19	43
BOOKS	57	100

I used to daydream about everyone at WCD knowing my name. And today, more than two dozen people said hi to me before I even got to my first-hour class. It made me happy to have so many new friends ☺.

In biology, we had to choose a lab partner and look at dust mites under a microscope. I thought for sure that Brandon was going to ask me to work with him. But three people interrupted him while he was trying to talk to me.

They were all like, "Hey, Nikki, let's work together so we can talk about my new tattoo design." But I didn't want to talk to people I hardly knew about tattoos. I wanted to have a really deep emo convo with Brandon about dust mites.

In the end, I got stuck with Alexis Hamilton, the

captain of the cheerleaders. The whole time we were working, all she did was blab about how they (the cheerleaders) needed me to come up with a "superhot" tattoo for their big game against Central, which, BTW, was on Friday.

But I already knew this because I overheard them talking about it in front of my locker this morning.

HEY...! WHERE'D SHE GO?!

A few of them were waiting around for me after second hour, and they seemed pretty cranky. It wasn't like I was afraid of them or anything; I just jumped inside my locker because I can be a little shy at times.

ME BEING HUNTED DOWN BY AN ANGRY MOB OF CHEERLEADERS!

Anyway, I told Alexis that everyone had to sign up with Zoey first. But she said Zoey had a waiting list of 149 people through next Wednesday, and she needed the tats right away since it was kind of an emergency. Alexis said she had already donated three books for each tattoo to Chloe, and Chloe was authorizing the squad to be placed at the top of the waiting list.

So, NOW it was *THREE books?!*

I told Alexis that since Zoey was director of scheduling and Chloe was director of book procurement, she should probably just ignore Chloe. Then Alexis got an attitude about the whole thing and refused to talk to me or help write our lab report on dust mites. Talk about a cruddy lab partner!

But what really upset me was that Zoey had scheduled 149 people without asking me first. I have a French test on Friday and a geometry test next Monday, and I'm barely pulling a C in each of those classes.

How am I supposed to study if I'm staying up past midnight EVERY night designing tats for all of these people?! And I haven't had time to eat lunch for the past two days!

Then, as I was leaving class, Samantha Gates stopped me to say how much she loved her tat of Justin Timberlake. She said all of her friends in the drama club wanted one too. She invited me to hang out with them after school on Friday, and I told her I'd let her know. But how can I have a social life when I have to draw tattoos 24/7? ☹!

THURSDAY, OCTOBER 3

	Today	Total
TATTOOS	33	76
BOOKS	99	199

I had a really CRUDDY day today! It seems that all Chloe, Zoey, and everyone cares about is TATTOOS.

I came to school early and did nine. Then I did fourteen at lunchtime and another ten during library. That's thirty-three tattoos!

Then I overheard Zoey tell Chloe, behind my back, that I worked "slower than a constipated snail in an ice storm," and I needed to speed up since she now had 216 people on the waiting list for next week. I was so NOT doing 216 tattoos in one week! And I told Zoey that right to her face. In a really friendly way.

Then Chloe wanted to know why I told Alexis to ignore her. She said that, since the cheerleaders had a big game, she thought they should be put at the top of the list for tomorrow. That's when Zoey said, as the director of scheduling, that the decision was hers alone and she didn't care what Chloe thought. Which was the EXACT same thing Chloe had said to us a few days ago.

Then Mrs. Peach came over and asked us to PLEASE lower our voices because we were, after all, in a library.

But I knew better. It WASN'T a library . . . !

IT WAS A WICKED
TATTOO SWEATSHOP! ☹

ME
(feeling very
miserable)

FRIDAY, OCTOBER 4

TATTOOS TODAY—A BIG FAT ZERO!

BOOKS TODAY—A BIG FAT ZERO!

WHY?

First of all, Chloe and Zoey were mad because I
didn't come to school early, and they had seventeen
people waiting for tattoos.

Well, excuuuuse me! But I had a French test today
that I had to study for.

Then, at lunch, there were twenty-five people
waiting. But instead of sitting at table 9 and
helping me, Chloe and Zoey sat at the CCP table on
the other side of the cafeteria.

I could see them giggling and acting all flirty with
Jason, Ryan, and Matt while I was supposed to
be working my butt off like CINDERELLA or
somebody!

But I nearly FREAKED when I saw MacKenzie give Chloe and Zoey INVITATIONS to her rescheduled party for next Saturday!

They were pink envelopes with big white satin ribbons tied around them, just like the one she had given ME.

And then taken back when she UNINVITED me!

Chloe and Zoey were acting all happy and sucking up to MacKenzie, even though they knew she HATED my guts.

SO I did the most mature and rational thing possible under the circumstances . . .

I QUIT ☹!

If I have to draw one more tattoo, I'm going to

VOMIT!

I thought Chloe and Zoey were my real friends.

But now I can see that they were just USING me all along to earn that trip to NYC for National Library Week.

HOW COULD THEY DO THIS TO ME?!

Then Brandon came up to my locker all smiley and said he wanted to interview me for the newspaper after school. But I told him to just forget it because my tattoo career was OVER! He asked me if I was okay, and I said, "Yeah, it's all good! I just need to find some new friends." He just blinked and looked kinda confused. Then he shrugged and walked away.

So now it's like CHLOE, ZOEY, and BRANDON are all TRIPPIN.'

I hope the three of them have a blast at MacKenzie's little party, since they all got invited and I DIDN'T!!

But it wasn't like I was jealous of them or anything. I mean, how totally juvenile would THAT be?!

I had the most horrible nightmare! It was like something out of the twilight zone.

MacKenzie was spitting bugs at me and all I could hear was the fifth-hour bell ringing and ringing.

IT WAS LIKE EVERYONE WAS OUT TO GET ME!!

Thank goodness I finally woke up. That's when I

realized it was morning and the telephone was ringing, not the fifth-hour bell. I dragged myself out of bed and answered the phone on my desk. It was my grandma calling to tell us she was planning to come visit us for two weeks at the end of the month. I told her my parents must already be out running errands or something since they hadn't answered the phone.

Then she asked me how I was doing, and I told her not so good. I said I was thinking about transferring out of my school and asked her what she would do if she were me. She said it was NOT so much about the school I chose, but whether I chose to be a chicken or a champion.

Which, of course, had ABSOLUTELY NOTHING to do with ANYTHING! Since Grandma was talking out of her head again, I told her that I loved her, but that I had to go because someone was at the door. Then I hung up.

I wasn't lying to her because, unfortunately, Brianna and Miss Penelope were at my bedroom door. Miss

Penelope wanted me to watch her do a medley of songs from *High School Musical 3* in the stylings of Amy Winehouse.

I had been awake for less than three minutes and had already been forced to deal with my senile grandma, my hyperactive sister, and a wacky puppet. I climbed back into bed, pulled the covers up over my head, and SCREAMED for two whole minutes.

So many FREAKS and not enough CIRCUSES!!

PLEASE, PLEASE, PLEASE make all of this NOT really be happening to me. Today has been the WORST day of my ENTIRE life!!

It all started Sunday night when I was sitting at my desk doing review problems for my geometry test.

My mom came into my room around midnight to tell me she was leaving the house extra early in the morning to chaperone a field trip for Brianna's class.

"Nikki, since you have a test and the art competition tomorrow, it's REALLY important that you set your alarm clock so you don't oversleep in the morning."

I was like, "Thanks, Mom. Good night!"

I really did plan to set my clock. As soon as I finished my geometry problems.

But the next thing I knew, it was morning and I was

STILL sitting at my desk with my geometry book open.

I just about had a heart attack because, according to my clock, it was 7:36 a.m. on MONDAY, and my first-hour class started at 8:00 a.m.!

The only logical explanation was that I must have fallen asleep while studying at my desk.

ME GETTING MY SNOOZE ON

(AND DROOLING ALL OVER MY GEOMETRY BOOK)

My day was off to a very bad start!

I had overslept, I didn't have a ride to school, my painting needed to be turned in for the art show, and my geometry test started in less than twenty-four, no, make that twenty-three, minutes.

Even the weather perfectly matched my miserable mood. It was dark, overcast, and pouring rain.

I was fighting back my tears when suddenly I heard the low rumble of our garage door opening. I ran to my bedroom window and spotted the flicker of bright headlights.

IT WAS MY DAD ☺! And he was leaving the house.

I rushed around my room in a panic, trying to get dressed before he pulled out. I jumped into my jeans and slid on my jacket. When I couldn't find one of my shoes, I decided to just change into my gym shoes once I got to school.

I grabbed my backpack and my painting and dashed

downstairs like a maniac. By the time I got out the front door, my dad was already pulling into the street.

I ran down our driveway, waving my arms and screaming hysterically.

"Wait, Dad! Wait! I overslept! I need a ride to school!"

Only, I couldn't run very fast because I was loaded down with my backpack and the painting. Of course, my bunny slippers didn't help the situation either.

Unfortunately, my dad DIDN'T see me! ☹

So I just stood there in our driveway in the pouring rain, feeling really, really cruddy. I couldn't believe I was going to miss the art show, receive an F on my geometry test, and get an unexcused absence, all in the same day. I got this large, painful lump in my throat, and I felt like crying again.

But my dad must have finally noticed me in his rearview mirror or something, because suddenly he slammed on his brakes. SKKKRREEEEECCHH! I took off running down the street toward the van as fast as I could.

As I climbed in, Dad chuckled. "Does Sleeping Beauty need a ride to school, or are you waiting for your prince?!"

I ignored his corny little joke and collapsed into the backseat of the van. I was soaking wet, but I felt happy and relieved. All was not lost! Yet, anyway.

But I also felt really anxious. For the first time this year, I was riding to school in the roachmobile!!

And if anyone saw me getting out of it, I was going to absolutely DIE!

By the time we pulled up to the front of the school, the rain had finally stopped. Thank goodness the only other vehicle around was a large truck with some men in uniform carrying in tall flat panels. I guessed that they were the displays for the art show.

I thanked Dad for the ride, grabbed my painting, and climbed out of the van. Just as I was about to slam the door shut, he waved and pointed to my backpack on the floor.

"Hey, I think you're forgetting something!"

I carefully set my painting on the ground and leaned it against the side of the van.

Then I climbed back in and grabbed my backpack.

"I think I'm all set now! Thanks again, Dad!"

I waved and slammed the van door shut.

I could NOT believe that I had actually made it to school in one piece with six minutes to spare. And not a single soul had spotted me getting out of the roachmobile, which was a miracle in and of itself.

Then I noticed a girl wearing matching Burberry raincoat, hat, and boots climbing out of the back of the truck parked in front of us.

"Hey, careful with that, buddy! It's a piece of art, not a piece of plywood!" she snarled at one of the men.

I froze and thought about trying to duck back into the van to hide until she left. But it was too late!

MacKenzie's mouth dropped open.

At first she had a look of shock on her face as

she stared at me, my van, and Max (yes, the roach). Then her lips spread into a really evil grin.

"Wait a minute! YOU'RE the same Maxwell as Maxwell's Bug Extermination?! And what is that hideous brown thing on top of your van, a dead horse?! Let me guess, it's supposed to be a matching set with those two dead bunnies on your feet?!"

I just glared at her and didn't say a word.

Okay, MacKenzie was the undisputed winner if we were competing for richest snob, cutest designer wardrobe, most friends, coolest bedroom, or biggest house.

But, we WEREN'T.

Avant-garde art was all about pure, unadulterated TALENT, which MacKenzie could NOT buy with her parents' money.

It was her Fab-4-Ever fashion illustrations against my watercolor . . .

And that was when I finally remembered my painting. I spun around and lunged to grab it just as my dad was pulling out.

But I was too late! I gasped and watched in horror as the van tire slowly crushed glass, antique wood frame, my hopes, and my dreams. It was shockingly painful to see the unique expression of me that had taken more than 130 hours to capture in watercolor so brutally destroyed in a matter of seconds.

But the torn, twisted, and splintered mess on

the side of the curb was not nearly as ugly as MacKenzie's final insult.

"Oh no! Was that your little art project?! Too bad! Hey, just throw some bugs on it and enter it as a modern art piece called *Maxwell's Bugs on Garbage*."

Then she cackled like a witch and sashayed off. I just HATED when MacKenzie sashayed!

I watched sadly as the roachmobile turned the corner and disappeared down the road.

For the first time in my life, I wished I were inside it, warm and dry and speeding away. Away from MacKenzie. Away from friends who were really NOT my friends. Away from Westchester Country Day Middle School.

I didn't fit in at this place, and I was sick and tired of trying. I sat down on the side of the curb, next to the pieces of my painting, and cried. The rain started to pour again, but I didn't care.

I had been sitting there like forever, trying to sort things out inside my head, when I noticed it had stopped raining. On ME, anyway.

Then, I recognized that faint aroma of Snuggle fabric softener, Axe body spray, and red licorice.

I looked up and was surprised and slightly embarrassed to see Brandon standing there holding an umbrella over me.

"You . . . okay?"

I didn't answer.

Then he extended his hand. I just looked at it and sighed. If I sat out on the curb in the cold rain much longer, I'd probably end up dying of pneumonia. Which, BTW, didn't sound like such a bad thing.

I grabbed ahold of his hand, and he slowly pulled me up off the wet curb.

I could NOT believe we were doing this stupid little scene all over again. How pathetic!

I rolled my eyes, sniffed, and wiped my runny nose on the back of my hand. I was NOT going to let him see me cry.

Both of us just stood there not saying anything. He was staring at me and I was staring at the ground.

Suddenly, Brandon dug deep into his pocket and fished out a wrinkled-looking piece of tissue.

"Um . . . I think you have . . . something on your face?"

"Probably SNOT!" I said sarcastically, and snatched the tissue from his hand.

"Yeah. Probably," he said, trying hard not to smile. "Like . . . I dig those shoes!"

"They're NOT shoes. They're bunny slippers! I was in a REALLY big hurry this morning, okay!"

I blew my nose at him loudly and angrily. HOOONKK!

"So . . . um, it looks like you had a little accident with your project."

"I wouldn't call it 'little.'"

"Well, if it will make you feel any better, MacKenzie is entering some life-size paper dolls. I'd say your painting is STILL better than hers. Even in twenty-seven pieces. With mud smeared on it. And a few worms."

A mischievous grin slowly spread across Brandon's face.

"Come on. Everyone knows you have more talent in your smallest burp than—"

"Yeah! I know. I KNOW . . . !" I said, interrupting him and blushing uncontrollably. I HATED when he did that to me!

Okay, even though I was mad at the world, I had to admit, this whole thing was a little funny. In a really bent sort of way.

Finally, I smiled at Brandon, and he winked at me. He was such a DORK! But in a good way. He had a slightly weird sense of humor and was friendly and a little shy ALL at the same time. And, unlike me, he didn't obsess about what other people thought about him. I think THAT was probably the coolest thing about him.

"Thanks for the umbrella!"

"Hey, no prob!"

Then we both walked to the front entrance.

256

Even though the building was warm, I felt really chilled.

My slippers were soaked, and it seemed like I was wearing sponges dipped in ice water on my feet.

"I need to get my shoes out of my locker and then go to the office to call my dad. Hopefully, he can drop off some dry clothing."

"So . . . I'll walk you to the office, if you don't mind. My class is on the way."

As Brandon and I made our way down the hall, some people stopped and stared, while others pointed and laughed. But I just ignored them.

I knew I looked pretty crazy. With every step I took, my bunny slippers went *sloshie-squeak, sloshie-squeak, sloshie-sqeak*, and left small puddles of water behind me.

When I finally got to my locker, there was a large crowd of kids gathered around it. At first I thought they were there for tattoos, but everyone quickly scattered.

Then I saw what they were looking at.

It felt like someone had punched me in my stomach so hard, I could hardly breathe. I covered my mouth and tried to blink back my tears for what seemed like the tenth time this morning.

Someone had written on my locker in what appeared to be Ravishing Red-Hot Cinnamon Twist lip gloss.

Which, BTW, was MacKenzie's favorite.

"I—I'm really sorry!" Brandon stammered. "Only a real loser would do something as mean and stupid as . . ."

But I didn't hear the rest of what he said.

I turned around, pushed my way through the crowded hallway, and went straight to the office to call my parents.

I couldn't take it anymore!

I was leaving Westchester Country Day Middle School.

And NEVER coming back!

Today I stayed home from school with a cold and just lounged in bed all day and drank lemon tea.

The Tyra Banks show rocked, as usual, but for some reason, it didn't cheer me up.

After my dad picked me up from school yesterday, I started thinking that maybe I was overreacting.

Watching my painting being smashed into a zillion pieces had been pretty traumatic, but it was mainly MacKenzie who was making my life miserable.

Maybe WCD wasn't such a horrible place. Maybe if I tried talking to Chloe and Zoey, we could go back to being friends again. Maybe Brandon hadn't written me off as a total loser.

So, on Monday afternoon, I called the library desk during fifth hour to talk to Chloe and Zoey.

Plus, I was a teensy bit curious about how

MacKenzie's art project had turned out. Okay, I admit, I was DYING to know! My hands were trembling as I dialed the phone.

"Library front desk, Zoey speaking."

"Hi, Zoey, it's me, Nikki. I was just calling to see how you guys are doing. You'd NEVER believe what happened to me this morning."

Then I heard Chloe's muffled voice in the background.

"OMG! It's her?! Just say you can't talk right now because we're really busy. We don't have time to waste."

"Um . . . what's up, Nikki? Brandon told us everything that happened. Actually, he's here right now. Too bad about your art project . . . ," Zoey stammered nervously.

"Yeah, I know. So, what are the three of you do—"

"Listen, Nikki, I really have to hang up now. We're really busy with, um . . . a project. Chloe and Brandon said hi."

"Wait, Zoey! I just wanted to—"

"Sorry, gotta go. See you tomorrow. Bye."

CLICK!

After that conversation, there was no doubt in my mind that Chloe, Zoey, and Brandon practically hated me. So there wasn't really anything left to do but make plans to transfer to a new school.

And have a really good CRY.

Which is what I've been doing on and off for the past twenty-four hours.

The only good thing

that's come out of all of this is that my parents have been so worried about my emotional state, they've finally agreed to let me transfer to the nearby public school.

I thanked my dad for arranging the scholarship and all, but unfortunately it just hadn't worked out.

Surprisingly, Mom and Dad took the news about their anniversary painting being destroyed really well.

I even promised I would paint them a new one, although Brianna insisted that she wanted to do it instead.

"Don't worry, Mom and Dad! I'm almost done making you a brand-new anniversary present, and it's way better than Nikki's dumb ol' painting!"

But I had a really bad feeling about Brianna's art project.

When I asked her if she had used finger paints or crayons, she said, "Nope! A black permanent marker.

And I drew it over the couch in the exact same spot where your painting was hanging!"

Brianna said her drawing was called . . .

THE MAXWELL FAMILY VISITS PRINCESS SUGAR PLUM ON BABY UNICORN ISLAND

When Mom saw Brianna's wall mural, she just about fainted. And then Brianna tried to get out of it by blaming Miss Penelope.

It was kind of nice to laugh again after feeling so hopelessly depressed.

My parents and I drove over to WCD forty-five minutes early so we could get everything taken care of before the students started arriving.

As Mom and Dad sat in the office chatting with the secretary and completing the school-transfer paperwork, I couldn't help noticing the colorful displays off the main entryway for the art competition.

No matter how much I tried to convince myself I didn't care, I just HAD to know if MacKenzie had won. It was like I was obsessed or something.

If I hurried, I could stop by the art competition for a few minutes and still have time to clean out my locker, get back to the office, and be out of the building before anyone spotted me.

"Well, I better get going," I muttered to my parents. I grabbed the empty cardboard box I had brought to carry the junk from my locker and headed down the hall.

The art exhibit was set up in the large student lounge near the cafeteria and was divided by grades. I hurried past the sixth- and seventh-grade displays to the eighth-grade section. There were about 24 entries, and I immediately spotted MacKenzie's.

Like everything she did, it was big, bold, and over the top. She had painted seven life-size mannequins dressed in her Fab-4-Ever fashions on six-foot-tall panels.

I had to admit, she was actually a pretty good fashion illustrator.

But the strange thing was that I didn't see her first-place ribbon.

Although, knowing MacKenzie, she probably had already taken it home so her parents could have it bronzed to match her baby shoes.

Then again, maybe NOT.

I was surprised to see the blue ribbon was hanging on the very last display.

I couldn't help pitying the poor artist who would have to put up with the drama over MacKenzie's very public and humiliating defeat.

The winning display was a series of sixteen 8 x 10 close-up black-and-white photographs of inked artwork.

When I read the title and artist's name, I almost

FREAKED OUT!

THE STUDENT BODY
BY NIKKI MAXWELL

I immediately recognized my tattoo artwork on Zoey's shoulder, Chloe's arm, Tyler's neck, Sophia's ankle, Matt's wrist, and on and on.

So _this_ must have been the "project" Chloe, Zoey, and Brandon were working on when they said they were too busy to talk to me on the telephone Monday afternoon.

Slowly but surely, the reality of the situation started to soak in.

I was like, "OMG! I WON first place in AVANT-GARDE ART! FIRST PLACE and five hundred dollars!"

Thanks to Chloe, Zoey, and Brandon! They must have cooked up this elaborate scheme after my painting got destroyed. And that fantabulous display with MY name on it had probably taken hours to complete.

I was SO wrong about them. They were the BEST friends EVER! And more than a dozen other kids had volunteered to be photographed. All of this totally BLEW MY MIND!

Maybe WCD was not such a horrible place after all. I actually had real friends here. And of course, it didn't hurt that I was now rich, rich, rich beyond my wildest dreams!

I hurried back to the office in a daze and burst inside.

"Mom, Dad! I've changed my mind. I want to stay!"

They both looked surprised.

"Honey, are you okay?" my mom asked, concerned.

"Actually, Mom, I'm GREAT! I've changed my mind. I want to stay. PLEASE!"

"Well, it's up to you. Are you sure?" my dad said, putting down his pen.

"I'm sure. I'm REALLY sure!"

The secretary gathered the papers from my dad, ripped them in half, and tossed them into the wastebasket.

"This is great news!" She beamed. "And congratulations on your first place in the art show! You're coming to the reception for the winners this Saturday, right? They'll be giving out the cash awards, and the catered dinner is fabulous."

My parents looked totally confused. "I thought you said you didn't—," my mom began, but I quickly interrupted her.

"Listen, I'll explain all of this later. Like, don't you both have somewhere to be?" I smiled and waved good-bye to them, hoping they would take the hint and get lost.

Mom kissed my forehead. "Okay, hon! We're glad you've decided to hang in there."

"Yeah, and you can thank Maxwell's Extermination for hooking you up!" my dad said, and winked. "I knew it would work out for you here, if you just gave it a chance."

"Well, I gotta go! Oh. Here, Dad!" I tossed him the cardboard box. "Can you get rid of this for me?"

Then I turned and rushed out of the office.

Students were starting to fill up the halls, and a few actually congratulated me. As I made my way back to my locker, I wasn't quite sure what to expect, but I was ready and willing to deal with it.

The graffiti had been cleaned up, thank goodness. But there was something new on my locker.

I knocked on the door of the janitor closet and then peeked inside.

Nikki,
Please meet us in the janitor's closet ASAP! It's very, very important!

Chloe and Zoey

271

Chloe and Zoey were sitting on the floor in a corner and looking pretty sad. I felt kind of sorry for them.

"We owe you an apology for the way we acted," Chloe said. "We got really carried away with all of the tattoo and book stuff. And that wasn't fair to you."

"Yeah! And we learned who our real friends are too. The CCPs wanted to hang out with us as long as you were doing the tattoos. What a bunch of phonies!" Zoey added.

"Actually, I kind of figured that out too. That angry mob of cheerleaders was too scary!" I said, shuddering at the memory.

"Listen, please don't be mad, Nikki!" Chloe said, starting to tear up. "But we have a confession to make . . ."

Zoey cleared her throat.

"Well, after we heard about the accident with your

painting, we rounded up the kids with your best tattoo artwork, and Brandon took pictures of them during lunch. Then he printed out the photographs on the computer in the newspaper office. Mrs. Peach let the three of us work on your entry the entire afternoon in the library. We called it *The Student Body.*"

"And you'll never guess what happened," Chloe sniffed, blinking back tears.

"I won!"

"YOU WON!!" they said together.

"Wait! You KNEW?!" Zoey asked, surprised.

"Yeah. I just found out a few minutes ago."

"We know we shouldn't have done it without asking you first. But there wasn't time. You're not mad at us, are you?" Chloe asked, and gave me jazz hands to try to lighten the mood.

"Actually, I am. I'm VERY ANGRY!" I hissed. Chloe and

Zoey both hung their heads and stared at the floor.

"We're sorry. We were just trying to help . . . ," Zoey muttered.

"You're supposed to be my friends. How could you two do this to me? I'm so TICKED! I would have given ANYTHING to have seen the look on MacKenzie's face when she LOST!" I was trying so hard not to laugh that I was starting to snort.

At first, both girls blinked and looked bewildered. Then, slowly, smiles spread across their faces until they were grinning from ear to ear.

"OMG! Nikki, you should have seen her," Chloe squealed. "When they announced you as the winner, she went into shock!"

"It was hilarious! MacKenzie threw a hissy fit right there in front of the judges!" Zoey snickered.

Pretty soon we were laughing and joking in the janitor's closest, just like old times.

"Uh-oh! I think I just heard the first bell," I groaned.

"Let's get out of here before we start smelling like a mildewy mop!"

Chloe and Zoey opened the door, and then stood there waiting for me to leave first.

"Talent before . . . brains!" Zoey winked and then gave me the stink eye.

"Talent before . . . beauty!" Chloe grinned and then gave me jazz hands.

"Hey, girlfriends, I see the talent! But, other than me, there's definitely no brains or beauty up in here!" I teased.

That's when Chloe and Zoey both socked me on my arm. "OW!!" I giggled. "That hurt!!"

There must have been a big sale at the mall yesterday or something, because four girls were wearing the exact same outfit.

I hadn't really noticed it until I overheard MacKenzie ridiculing them in the hall.

"OMG! Look at that! They're ALL wearing the same butt–ugly ensemble! Wait, don't tell me. They were giving them away for free with a purchase of a McDonald's Happy Meal!"

It was only 7:45 a.m., and I was already visualizing duct tape over her mouth.

When MacKenzie finally noticed me, she tried to act all innocent.

"Just in case you're wondering, I DIDN'T write 'Bug Girl' on your locker. Lots of people wear Ravishing Red–Hot Cinnamon Twist, you know."

I just rolled my eyes at her. That girl is SUCH a liar! I didn't believe her for one second.

MacKenzie flipped her hair and gazed at her perfect image in her mirror.

"Besides, even if I did it, you don't have any proof!"

Then she applied her morning layer of lip gloss.

Since I was stuck having a locker next to MacKenzie's for the rest of the year, I decided to utilize the mind-over-matter coping strategy that Zoey had developed.

In my MIND, I was so OVER being impressed with MacKenzie, because she didn't MATTER!

Although, I have to admit, those hoop earrings she was wearing were to die for.

Why is it that huge dangly earrings look really GLAMTASTIC on the CCP girls? But when normal girls (like me) wear them, we end up needing reconstructive cosmetic surgery.

POPULAR GIRL IN
BIG DANGLY EARRINGS

UNPOPULAR GIRL IN
BIG DANGLY EARRINGS

Zoey, Chloe, and I sat together at lunch at table 9, and a lot of people stopped by to ask about tattoos. Since our Ink Exchange Program was such a big hit, and we had already collected almost two hundred books for charity, we decided to continue it for just three days each month, starting in November. It was going to be great NOT having to hide inside my locker between classes, due to my fear of angry mobs—I mean, my shyness.

But the strangest thing was that I was actually starting to look forward to attending National Library Week at the NYC public library. And we had a good chance of being selected. I mean, just think about it! Chloe, Zoey, and me in Manhattan for five days without our 'rents! How EXCITING would THAT be?!

We were going to have Friends, Fun, Fashion, Food & Flirting like it says in *That's So Hot!* magazine. And maybe even get tickets to the

TYRA BANKS SHOW!

I just LOVE that GIRL!!

I also planned to take full advantage of the "Meet-n-Greet" with all those famous authors. I had no idea an autographed novel was so valuable.

I planned to collect a half dozen and then sell them on eBay for big bucks. Then, KA-CHING!! I could buy that iPhone I've been wanting! Am I NOT brilliant?! ☺!

BTW, I decided to save the $500 prize money for art camp next summer. It was going to be my fifth year attending, and my instructor said I already had an art portfolio strong enough for college. Which is pretty fantastic, seeing as I'm not even in high school yet! She said if I continued to work really hard, I could maybe land a four-year scholarship to a major university. *SWEET!*

Brandon stopped by our table to ask if he could interview me about winning the avant-garde art competition, since it was "breaking news."

I thanked him for taking the photographs of my tattoo designs and told him what a great job he had done on them. But he said it was no biggie, and he planned to use the photos for the article he was writing.

Then MacKenzie came over, acting all friendly, and actually congratulated me. I was so shocked, I almost puked my lunch on her Jimmy Choos!

But I think she really just wanted to flirt with Brandon, because she kept batting her eyes at him all fluttery, like she had accidentally stuck a false eyelash to her eyeball or something.

How does she have the nerve to do that right to my face?! Probably because she has the IQ of lint.

In spite of the fact that we had agreed not to do any tattoos until next month, Chloe and Zoey insisted that I do just ONE more . . .

FOR MYSELF.

My tattoo totally ROCKED!

Okay, I admit I was wrong about Grandma being senile. But I was correct about that DEMENTED puppet, Miss Penelope.

After lunch was over, Brandon walked with me to biology class. He brushed the hair out of his eyes with his fingers (again) and smiled at me kind of shylike.

"So I . . . um . . . was wondering if . . . um . . . you wanted to be lab partners for 'structure of mitochondria'?"

I could NOT believe he asked me that. So I looked deep into his eyes, all serious, and said:

"WHEEEEEEEEEEEEEEEEEE!!"

I'm sure he thought I was CRAZY.

But, hey! I can only be myself, right?

I'M SUCH A DORK!
☺!!!